P9-DLZ-527

Unspeakable Women

Unspeakable Women

Women

SELECTED SHORT STORIES
WRITTEN BY ITALIAN WOMEN
DURING FASCISM

TRANSLATIONS, INTRODUCTION, AND AFTERWORD BY
ROBIN PICKERING-IAZZI

THE FEMINIST PRESS at The City University of New York • New York

©1993 by Robin Pickering-Iazzi
All rights reserved
Published 1993 by The Feminist Press at The City University of New York, 311 East 94 Street, New York, NY 10128

97 96 95 94 93 5 4 3 2 1

Library of Congress Cataloging-in-Publication Data

Unspeakable women : selected short stories written by Italian women
    during Fascism / translations, introduction, and afterword by Robin
    Pickering-Iazzi.
        p. cm.
    ISBN 1-55861-062-6 (cloth) : $35.00. — ISBN 1-55861-063-4 (paper)
: $14.95
    1. Italian fiction—Women authors—Translations into English.
2. Short stories, Italian—Translations into English.   3. Italian
fiction—20th century—Translations into English.   4. Women—Italy—
Fiction.   I. Pickering-Iazzi, Robin Wynette.
PQ4257.E5U67   1993
853'.01089287—dc20   93-13534
                                                                    CIP

Permissions acknowledgments are on page xvi.

This publication is made possible, in part, by public funds from the New York State Council on the Arts and the National Endowment for the Arts. The Feminist Press is also grateful to Joanne Markell and Genevieve Vaughan for their generosity.

Text and cover design: Paula Martinac
Cover art: Anna E. Meltzer (1896–1974), *Woman at Window,* 1939. Oil on canvas, 36 x 26". Reproduced courtesy of Janet Marqusee Fine Arts, Ltd.

Typeset by: The Type Set, New York, New York.
Printed in the United States of America on acid-free paper by
McNaughton & Gunn, Inc., Saline, Michigan.

*To Rebecca Workman, Ada Blankenship,
Norma Pickering, and Maria Stella Iazzi*

Contents

Chronological Listing of Short Stories

Preface

Most of us are familiar with the "Italian Woman" of popular American culture: with few exceptions, she is the all-sacrificing "mamma" of sitcoms and films, or perhaps the exotic object of male desire made famous by Sophia Loren in Hollywood movies. These female models are not all that different from those propagandized by the Fascist dictatorship in Italy during the 1920s and 1930s, despite the distinct conditions in which they were produced. The "New Woman" of Italian Fascism was to embody the ideal of female self-sacrifice, whether in her role as the supreme wife and mother or as sexual object for the "New Man," aggrandizing male virility. The short stories I have translated for this collection challenge these myths today, as they did when originally published, by making us see the different identities and desires that modern Italian women perceived, created, and imagined for themselves, even in the face of an especially authoritarian regime.

This volume features short stories written by award-winning and widely read Italian women authors between 1925 and 1939, during the years of the Fascist dictatorship and before Italy's entrance into the Second World War. While the authors' names and literature may be unfamiliar to most contemporary readers of English, they were explosively popular in Italy. The literary accomplishments of such writers as Grazia Deledda, recipient of the 1926 Nobel Prize for Literature, Amalia Guglielminetti, Gianna Manzini, Ada Negri, Carola Prosperi, and Clarice Tartufari also earned the recognition of esteemed critics of their day. In view of these authors' significance in Italian culture of the twenties and thirties, it is astonishing that this volume is the first of its kind in English. For that matter, such a collection has yet to be published in Italy, a fact that reveals much about how marginalized Italian women's literature of this period has been.

My own discovery of this fascinating period of women's literature dates back to 1983 when I began the research for my dissertation, a critical examination of the short fiction contributed to the cultural page, also known as the "third page," of Italian newspapers from 1920 to 1960. Though few studies had been written about the cultural page, an institution unique to Italian journalism, the classic work *Nostra "terza pagina"* (Our "third page") by Enrico Falqui provided historical information profiling a long list of internationally acclaimed and popular male writers who published fiction in the daily press. Thus, when I began to read editions dating from the teens to the seventies of the *Corriere della sera* (Evening messenger), *Il giornale d'Italia* (The newspaper of Italy), and *La stampa* (The press) (each nationally distributed dailies published respectively in Milan, Rome, and Turin), I anticipated finding short stories by such major figures as Luigi Pirandello, Alberto Moravia, and Dino Buzzati, as well as selections by Grazia Deledda and Ada Negri, who were mentioned in Falqui's study. But I was not prepared to uncover hundreds of short stories written by a variety of renowned and popular women authors.

As more copies of Italian newspapers of the 1920s and 1930s arrived at the Interlibrary Loan office, my list of women writers contributing fiction to the cultural page grew along with the number of short stories preserved on microfilm or printed on the disintegrating pages of old newspapers. The very existence of this imposing body of women's writing posed the first of many contradictions to conventional accounts of life and culture during the Fascist regime. Most literary histories and anthologies omitted women altogether, some citing the ubiquitous repression of women in the rigid Fascist hierarchy. Others alleged that female authors "reproduced" patriarchal models of woman, particularly those of the wife and mother or the vamp. Yet, in spite of the oppressive measures taken to stifle women's public voices in the regime, significant numbers of female authors published their fiction on the highly esteemed cultural page. Furthermore, the stories women told—many of which explicitly critiqued traditional models of femininity—explored such crucial issues as female gender roles, sexuality, identity, and creativity. Ironically, the repression of women's literary voices of the twenties and thirties was accomplished not by the Fascists, but by the sexual politics shaping postwar literary debates in liberal democratic Italy. Indeed, the contribution such writers as Deledda, Negri, Tartufari, and Guglielminetti made to Italian life and culture during the dictatorship had been almost entirely omitted from postwar anthologies and literary criticism on the interwar period.

By acquainting contemporary readers with literature by some of Italy's most talented female authors, this collection should put to rest the notion that women's writing of this period is of marginal value. These short stories have far-reaching implications for how we think about women during the Italian Fascist regime and perhaps other dictatorships because they restore the vital distinction between the concept of the "New Woman" in Fascist ideology and the ideas of self and female experience articulated by women themselves. Women's fiction and its success among general readers and critics suggest cultural prominence, not absence; struggle, not resignation; self-expression, not silence. In their transgression of Fascist strictures and contradiction of contemporary cultural histories, these stories force us to see Italian women and their writing through very different eyes.

Acknowledgments

Throughout this project I have benefited from the support of many friends, colleagues, and students. I owe particular gratitude to Pia Friedrich, who has been a valued mentor to me. The expertise she brought to her reading of the short stories in Italian and English enriched the translations, while preventing errors. I thank Laura Roscos for her editing of the stories in draft form, and Martine Meyer, Stephanie Meyer, and Amy Stone for their comments on later versions of the translations. Many of the suggestions Beverly Allen offered for "Baptisms" have been adopted in the text. Anna Monardo's editorial work helped polish the stories in English. Fiora Bassanese and Thomas Piontek gave me insightful advice on the Afterword. Kate Kramer provided research support, locating many materials needed for this project. I have also appreciated the questions and observations shared by students in my courses on Italian women writers and Italian Fascism. I gratefully acknowledge the different forms of institutional support that have facilitated my work. The University of Wisconsin-Milwaukee Graduate School funded my research in Italy. The University of Wisconsin-Milwaukee Center for Twentieth Century Studies, under the direction of Kathleen Woodward, deserves particular mention for creating congenial space and time for me to write during my tenure as Fellow in 1989-90. The College of Letters and Science of the University of Wisconsin-Milwaukee also provided financial support for preparation of the manuscript, which Julie Liotta patiently typed. I am grateful to

Florence Howe, Susannah Driver, and Kathy Casto, who have offered creative solutions for unique problems throughout the phases of manuscript preparation and production.

I especially wish to voice my gratitude to Paolo Iazzi for his discussions of the ideas in this book, and for the many other ways he untiringly provided intellectual and personal support, and to Andrè Iazzi for the patience and understanding he showed while I was preparing this volume.

I am indebted to the following authors and newspapers for permission to translate and print the following selections in this collection. Grazia Deledda: "Battesimi" and "Ritratto di contadina" by permission of the *Corriere della sera*—Milan, Italy. Ada Negri: "La Capitana," "Il cinematografo," and "Signora con bambina" by permission of the *Corriere della sera*—Milan, Italy. Carola Prosperi: "Fuori del labirinto" by permission of Editrice La Stampa S.p.A.—Turin, Italy.

Unspeakable Women

Introduction

So long as the mother speaks the language she must speak, our
children will see Fascism . . . as the only idea worthy of being loved
and served.
                    —"The Woman Mother in Fascism," *Critica fascista*, 1931

And I was caught in the circle of faith and fantasy of the little woman
who blindly believed in the power of the written word, a power
nonetheless that can truly span centuries and infinite spaces, and
reach from the beggar to the king, if it springs from the pure of
heart.
                    —Grazia Deledda, "Grace," 1933

*I*t would be difficult to identify a place and time in history that has
generated more fascination and controversy than Italy during the years
of Fascism. The sheer volume of studies written on a broad spectrum
of issues relating to life, culture, and society in Mussolini's regime makes
the relative silence on the subject of literature written by Italian wom-
en during this period all the more conspicuous. With this and the especially patriarchal and repressive character of the regime in mind it
may seem improbable for many readers—as it did for me—that Italian
women exercised their power as writers to speak of themselves in ways
never voiced before. In the twenties and thirties, however, the number
of women writing in Italy notably increased, as they published novels
and contributed poetry and fiction to literary journals, magazines, local and nationally distributed newspapers, and the booming women's
press. While commanding the sustained attention of the emergent mass
readership, the literature written by women also received noteworthy
critical acclaim among prominent figures in the literary establishment.
The continued publication of prose works by Gianna Manzini (1896–
1974) and Grazia Deledda (1871–1936), the 1926 recipient of the Nobel
Prize for Literature, testifies to the contemporary interest in these writers

among Italian readers. Yet, apart from rare appearances in anthologies, literary works by Amalia Guglielminetti (1881–1941), Ada Negri (1870–1945), Carola Prosperi (1883–?), and Clarice Tartufari (1868–1933) —once applauded for their innovation of content and style—must be sought in aging editions.[1] The short fiction by such popular writers as Maddalena Crispolti, Marinella Lodi, and Pia Rimini is available only on microfilm or the yellowing pages of the newspapers and magazines to which these women contributed in the years of Fascism. (And biographical information about them is not available at all.) This collection is the first to make a sampling of short stories written by some of the most artful practitioners of the genre during Fascism available for contemporary readers. The selections have never been published together in Italian, nor have they been translated into English.

Reasons why critics have neglected women's literature written during Fascism primarily concern the oppressive political practices instituted by the Fascist dictatorship to manage the forms of life, society, and culture.[2] Italian Fascism was a political movement that, with Benito Mussolini (1883–1945) as its founder and chief, ruled Italy from October 28, 1922 to July 25, 1943. The Fascist movement began in a period of social upheaval following the First World War, when shortages of fuel, food, and housing, high unemployment and underemployment, as well as strikes in urban and rural areas were facts of everyday life. With promises of social order, economic stability, and national greatness, the Fascist party made its appeal primarily to war veterans, students with few prospects of employment, young professionals, landowners, and industrialists. Although this new political group had few followers in 1919, numbering some 870 members, by the end of 1921 it boasted approximately 250,000 members.[3] Correspondingly, Fascist squads of "blackshirts," a paramilitary force, expanded their spheres of activity from primarily urban industrial sites to rural areas, quashing with physical violence the increased bargaining power the working classes had achieved in Socialist organizations and peasant leagues. Although it is impossible to define what Alexander De Grand aptly termed the "composite ideology" of Italian Fascism—indeed Mussolini stated that he invented Fascism anew each day—its proponents generally opposed the liberal democratic tradition of Italian politics, Socialism, the feminist movement, and clearly, multiparty systems of government.

A politics of repression remained a fundamental characteristic of Italian Fascism throughout the dictatorship, despite the semblance of legitimacy achieved on Mussolini's entrance into power in October of 1922. Following the March on Rome, when Mussolini mobilized his Fascist squads and brought parliamentarians to loggerheads over a course of action, King Victor Emmanuel III made the Fascist leader prime minister of Italy. While working within the parliamentary system for the first two years of his appointment, Mussolini began to enact measures that gave him exceptional, and ultimately dictatorial, powers. Among these measures were the formation of the Voluntary Militia for National Security and the secret police (OVRA), the establishment of the Fascist Grand Council as the sole policy-making body, the creation of the Special Tribunal for trying political cases, the outlawing of oppositional political parties, and the abolishment of freedom of the press. Furthermore, a gamut of domestic policies and organizations—for instance, youth and leisure time organizations, and the National Agency for Maternity and Childhood (ONMI)—politicized the "private," endeavoring to fascitize the family as the smallest unit of this authoritarian regime, whose motto was "Believe, Obey, Fight."[4]

Not surprisingly, the conservative scope of Fascist politics, which most oppressed the working classes in defense of dominant interest groups, doubly marginalized women. Thus, postwar literary commentary has tended to equate the repression of women's voices in the "official" spheres of Italian politics with repression of their literary voices. To be sure, the Fascist ideology of woman and policies enacted to reinstitute the traditionally defined female role of exemplary wife and mother were intended to contain women's other pursuits. Among the first acts of repression taken to deflate women's increasing political activism was to stall the introduction of a woman's suffrage bill into parliament, where the women's vote had gained substantial support. In 1925 Mussolini granted administrative voting rights in local elections to limited groups of women, but voting became a moot question in 1926, when he assumed full dictatorial powers. At the same time, Fascist ideologues propagandized the model of wife and mother, fashionably called the "New Woman," as the exclusive means to fulfilling women's political, social, and "natural" mission in the totalitarian state. They thus recodified past theories of biological essentialism. The image of the "New Woman"—shapely, prolific, and therefore physically, emotionally, and sexually healthy—was increasingly publicized in speeches, ceremonies dedicated to mothers of large families, posters, and pamphlets following Mussolini's Ascension Day Speech of May 26, 1927, which established the demographic campaign as the matrix of Fascist sexual politics. Yet, different visual images of modern Italian women studying, working, and challenging traditional gender boundaries continued to circulate in such daily newspapers as the *Corriere della sera* and *La stampa*, and in such women's publications as *Almanacco della donna italiana* (Italian woman's almanac).

Propaganda was not Mussolini's only tool: The regime also implemented punitive and incentive policies to regulate women's access to higher education and employment outside the home. With the ostensible aim of doubling the Italian population, the measures enacted to restrict female actions and influence to the home also addressed the concerns of dominant interest groups about male unemployment, the crisis of the traditional family structure, and the loss of male authority.

As recent historical studies on women in the Italian Fascist regime have shown, it is difficult to gauge the effectiveness of Fascist propaganda and policies on women's sense of identity, ideas, and occupations.[5] For instance, trends in education and employment among urban women of the popular and middle classes point to contradictions between their concerns, interests, and pursuits and those prescribed in the Fascist notion of the "New Woman." As part of a program initiated in the twenties to reduce the overall number of students competing for limited technical and professional positions, female students were required to pay higher instructional fees. Although unsuccessful, attempts were later made to develop a special home economics curriculum for women students, which would suit "female" intellectual capabilities and the responsibilities necessary for educating children and household governance. Despite the general decline in university enrollments, which was also influenced by men's entrance into the armed forces, the percentages of female students showed steady, albeit slow, increases until the period between 1935 and 1942, when the numbers of women attending Italian universities rose more rapidly from 17.4 percent to 29.9 percent (Alexander De Grand, "Women under Italian Fascism," 960). Besides maintaining a strong presence in such traditionally female areas of study as teaching, nursing, and literature, women began to enter male-dominated disciplines, including law, political science, medicine, and physics.

Women's own ways of speaking about education during the regime show a sustained commitment to achieving intellectual and economic independence. In a 1930 article published in the women's journal *Giornale della donna* (The woman's magazine), one woman counters the Fascist argument attributing Italy's declining birthrate to a feminist desire for education, stating: "According to us feminism does not even enter into the desire of women to educate themselves, to better themselves, to act independently. If possibly it is a consequence, it is not the cause of such desires. It is born when the necessity arises to defend and further women's work, which has been discouraged and denigrated only because it is done by women" (De Grand, 963). Testimonies from female adolescents, gathered eight years later, raise further doubts regarding the effectiveness of Fascist campaigns to instill female self-sacrifice and motherhood as women's sole personal, social, and political ideal. Professor Spolverini, the director of an Italian pediatric clinic, reported in 1938 that the foremost desire young girls expressed to their doctors was not to have a husband and children, but to get an education and a well paying position in order to "be self-sufficient . . . and lead an intellectually and economically independent life" (Piero Meldini, *Sposa e madre esemplare* [The exemplary wife and mother], 263).[6] Similarly, the ideas of one thousand Roman schoolgirls between the ages of sixteen and eighteen tell us that young women in urban areas may have aspired to something other than being the guardian angel of hearth and family. In 1937 Maria Gasca Diez, then director of Rome's Institute for Professional Orientation and in 1944 a member of the Italian Women's Union, a largely leftist organization advocating for women's rights, conducted a survey among these adolescents, who had grown up during Fascism. The results of the interviews, published in 1938, indicated that only 10 percent had any interest in domestic responsibilities and 27 percent hated them. Very few wanted a large family (the clear preference being to have one child, or two at the most), and the majority of girls voiced the wish to command rather than obey (Meldini, 263–4).

Although more psychologically and materially oppressive, the measures enacted to reduce female employment also achieved complex results. Building on trends originating in the late 1800s, Italian women had made notable advances in socioeconomic mobility in urban sites through the early 1900s, a process accelerated by World War I. As Lucia Birnbaum (1986) notes in her historical study *Liberazione della donna: Feminism in Italy,* numbers of women from economically depressed rural areas moved to find work in rice and tobacco fields, in machine factories, and in the clothing industry, while women of the middle classes occupied positions in the private and public sectors as bookkeepers, typists, secretaries, teachers, nurses, and journalists. Exponents of Fascism deployed psychological tactics to scare these women out of the work force. Doctors, psychiatrists, criminologists, and economists devoted exceptional attention in their writings to propagandizing a gamut of deleterious "symptoms" that would afflict working women, particularly those of the middle classes. These include dissatisfaction with domestic responsibilities, alienation toward pregnancy, sterility, masculinization, and changes in sexual orientation. Moreover, policies were implemented to decrease the numbers of women employed in or entering the work place. These range from discriminatory hiring directives, which in 1929 gave preference to men with children, to legislated restrictions on women's access to employment. In 1938, for example, two decrees were passed, one limiting to 10 percent the number of women employed as teachers in higher education, the other restricting female employees in private and government projects to 10 percent. Yet, according to De Grand loopholes, inconsistent hiring practices, and

Italy's entrance into the Second World War stymied both programs. The complexity of assessing the ways repressive or protective policies influenced women's everyday lives is perhaps best illustrated by the reduction of women's wages, which had a double edge. As Meldini argues, this measure may have deterred some women from working, but it also made female workers—many of whom worked out of necessity—all the more in demand among employers looking for cheap labor. In like manner, the protective legislation enacted for working mothers in the thirties did improve women's working conditions by providing for extended compulsory maternity leave, the right to return to the job up to six weeks following delivery, breaks for infant feeding, and the establishment of on-site feeding rooms in companies with more than fifty female employees. But, as Lesley Caldwell (1986) suggests in "Reproducers of the Nation," such legislation may also have deterred potential employers from hiring women of childbearing age.

Clearly, a complex variety of factors such as class, age, and geographic location influenced women's choices regarding work and childbearing. However, trends in female employment during Fascism, as well as the testimonies of working women, contradict the notion that the repressive sexual politics of the regime immobilized women's abilities to act on aspirations, ideals, and enterprises other than marriage and motherhood. According to the studies by De Grand and Meldini, the numbers of women employed in several sectors—domestic services, commerce, finance, administration, health care, and teaching—increased, sometimes markedly, during the twenties and thirties.

Women provide the most authoritative voice on the significance working outside the home may have had during the dictatorship. The oral testimonies examined by Luisa Passerini (1987) in *Fascism in Popular Memory* record that women of the Turin working class thought of themselves as the subjects of their own lives who, by making the decisions to be employed in the workplace and to have fewer children, achieved progress in relation to their mothers' generation. Employment also figures prominently in oral narratives of middle-class women working as secretaries, typists, and teachers. For these women, Passerini indicates, "work seemed to offer not only material independence but also the primary basis for a psychological and social identity, despite relative indifference, especially among clerical workers, toward the content of the job" (50). Considering these different forms of female identity among real women, it should come as no surprise that Fascist speeches appealing to women only as mothers alienated certain sectors of the female population. Tosca, a woman of the Turin working class recalls, "Oh Fascism! The Duce! Have babies! Don't think about your husband, have babies, give me babies to slaughter. He only wanted boys. To make war. Then he made it" (Passerini, 150). In some cases, women interviewed by Passerini think of their decision to limit family size as political resistance to the demographic campaign. Here are Fiora's comments:

> How many children did you have?
> *Fiora:* I had three.
> Are they alive?
> *Fiora:* Yes, yes. They're all alive. I would have had more, but you didn't to spite Mussolini, you see. (150)

However, the complex variety of cultural, socioeconomic, political, and religious conditions shaping women's diverse experiences of Fascism in different Italian communities makes it impossible to generalize from such testimonies.

Despite the coercive and punitive mechanisms deployed to repress female voices in the Fascist regime, women writers made a prominent space for themselves in Italian life and society, challenging masculine culture by devoting sustained attention to women's lives as a valuable subject for literary creation, and to creating their own forms of expression. The need to deflate women writers' threat to patriarchal order was perceived by Gherardo Casini, who in 1929 cautioned the readers of *Critica fascista* (Fascist critique) that "It will be to our credit if we can extend the restraints we've applied to women in politics to other fields, above all to art and literature" (Meldini, 168). Although Fascist politicians did not develop a *systematic* cultural policy to repress literature by women, or to curtail its circulation, female authors were the object of a campaign conducted primarily in Fascist publications, which was designed to domesticate their writing. While assailing the legitimacy of women's claim to literary authority—since it was alien to the patriarchal concept of female biological, social, and political destiny—Fascist thinkers constructed the model of the intellectual woman as an "unnatural," masculinized, diseased, and empty figure. According to the literary critic Luigi Tonelli, "Woman must be encouraged to live right, not to write literature. She must be helped to be a good wife and exemplary mother, not to become an empty and useless 'celebrity' . . . this is passé, I know, but man's future rests in the sweet and sorrowful lap of Mary, not in the sterile and furious one of Sappho, or Aurora Dupin" (*Almanacco della donna italiana* III (3) 1922: 239). The exchanges between sociopolitical statements and literary criticism were rarely so overt during Fascism; however, Tonelli's paternalistic recommendation clearly summarizes the sexual politics operating to guide women away from the traditionally male preserve of literary production.

Although Fascist admonitions did not prevent women writers' critical and popular success, even such acclaimed authors as Deledda and Negri speak of tragic contradictions and marginality in their lives as literary women. In "Grace," for instance, Deledda describes personal struggles to overcome the unrelenting "persecution"—both "frightening and dangerous"—of family, community, and the critical establishment, which is provoked by her nonconformist choice to be a writer. Born and raised in the insular, tight-knit community of Nuoro in Sardinia, Deledda was in fact ostracized, when at fifteen she began publishing her writing. Negri articulated a similar awareness of women's uneasy relation to literary production in a 1925 interview. Posing the question of what it meant to be a female author, Negri revealed she "always thought a woman writer was a man condemned to live in a woman's body."[7] This statement reflects the general notion of creativity as a "masculine" trait, which still had currency in Italy and elsewhere during the twenties and thirties.

In some instances the regime did voice opposition to individual women writers. For example, Pia Rimini's name appears on a lengthy list of authors of whom the Fascist regime disapproved in 1940. Since so little is known about Rimini, we can only speculate about how this may have affected her writing and career. From the late thirties until her death in 1942, the novelist Annie Vivanti was a prohibited subject for newspaper coverage.[8] Yet Benedetto Croce published a positive assessment of her literary works in 1940, in *La letteratura della nuova Italia* VI (Literature of the new Italy). Similarly, the regime took a hostile stand toward Alba De Céspedes, claiming that her writing did not reflect the "Fascist ethic." Given the popular attraction to what is censored or prohibited, this position may have contributed to this writer's success. De Céspedes' 1938 novel, *Nessuno torna indietro* (trans. *There's No Turning Back*), sold over 150,000 copies by 1943.

During Fascism the poetry, novels, and romance fiction by women writers generated unprecedented popularity among a mass readership. Deledda, Guglielminetti, Negri, and Prosperi all had bestselling novels and poetry collections in this period.[9] More surprisingly, female writers represented a formidable presence on the cultural page of Italian dailies specifically during the years of Fascist rule.[10] Along with such internationally acclaimed male authors as Dino Buzzati, Eugenio Montale, Alberto Moravia, and Luigi Pirandello, established and new women writers contributed short fiction to this forum. Each of the short stories in this collection, with the exception of "Grace" by Deledda, was originally published on the cultural page of nationally distributed newspapers: the *Corriere della sera* of Milan, *Il giornale d'Italia* of Rome, or *La stampa* of Turin. I have selected the fiction from this source because women's contribution of literature to the cultural page, which has been overlooked by scholars, has particular importance for understanding the role of female authors in Italian life and society during the dictatorship. Certainly the economic benefits of publishing fiction in the press provided some women with the means to support themselves as professional writers. More significantly, by publishing their short stories on the cultural page, women writers were able to speak to an economically and socially diversified community of readers, some of whom they might otherwise not have reached since the price of books was still prohibitive for many Italians.[11] For example, by 1943 Negri's autobiography, *Stella mattutina* (Morning star), which was a critical and popular success, had sold sixty thousand copies since its publication in 1921, while during the 1930s, the fiction she published in the *Corriere della sera* could reach over 600,000 readers per day. The wide circulation and success of women's fiction belie the notion that women writers represented a marginal cultural force during the interwar period.

In the Fascist years women writers comprised a visible and vocal presence on the esteemed cultural page, whose configurations changed as different female authors contributed fiction with varying frequency. Beginning in the mid-twenties, Negri and Deledda regularly contributed short fiction and essays to the *Corriere della sera*, while continuing to write in other genres. Deledda, who also published a few pieces in *Il giornale d'Italia*, contributed well over one hundred short stories from 1923 until she died in 1936, and Negri published some eighty short narratives between 1926 and 1942. Whereas the *Corriere della sera* relied more upon established authors, *Il giornale d'Italia* frequently opened its cultural page to popular women writers, while also featuring short fiction by such critically recognized figures as Guglielminetti, Manzini, and Tartufari. From 1924 through 1939 more than twenty women authors—including Astaldi, Crispolti, Lodi, and Rimini—published their literature in this Roman daily.[12] In the 20s and 30s, readers of *La stampa* could anticipate three to four short stories per month by Carola Prosperi, as well as fiction by Rimini and Guglielminetti, among others. Although the cultural page featured more writing by men than women, it is remarkable that works by female authors were published in this public, influential forum in the authoritarian Fascist regime, where, in Mussolini's words, "women do not count."

To give readers an idea of the personal and professional diversity among women writers contributing literature to major Italian newspapers during Fascism, I have chosen works by both critically recognized and popular authors who represent different generations, socioeconomic classes, political orientations, and geographic locations. Among the generation of established authors who had witnessed the political activism of the working classes and the women's emancipation movement (from the late 1800s through the early 1900s) are Clarice Tartufari, Grazia Deledda, Ada Negri, Carola Prosperi, and Amalia Guglielminetti. Born in Rome in 1868, Tartufari married young, and began her literary career as a poet in 1894 with the collection *Nuovi versi* (New verses). But it was her skill as a novelist that earned sustained critical attention, beginning in 1909 with the publication of *Il miracolo* (The miracle), the first of eleven novels. In 1940 Benedetto Croce, a preeminent critic of the time, applauded Tartufari for her deft portrayals of the ideas, attitudes, and manners of everyday life in its personal and social dimensions. Her attentive description of physical settings and social milieus is amply illustrated in "A Life Story?" which records the author's mature reflections on writing histories of female subjects, generally excluded from the history of politics and society written by and for men, a relevant theme today. The strong female protagonists Tartufari created in her novels and short stories, and her analysis of power relations between the sexes, were pioneering for the time. Although Tartufari died in 1933, she was an important figure in cultural life during Fascism. During this period she published four of her best novels, wrote fiction for the daily press, and was an assiduous contributor to women's publications.

Deledda's life story and her breadth of literary success, unrivaled by most female and male writers of her time, make her an extraordinary figure. As described in "Grace" and in her autobiography, *Cosima*, published posthumously in 1937, Deledda grew up in Nuoro, a town rigidly structured by patriarchal beliefs, customs, and traditions. The town's location, in the mountainous inner regions of Sardinia, isolated the community from the socioeconomic and political changes occurring on the peninsula.[13] In 1871, when Deledda was born, Nuoro had no railroad or telegraph services. Girls could not leave their houses unless escorted by an adult family member and, as in Deledda's case, they could neither be seen in public nor appear by a window during mourning for a family member. Deledda's middle-class family saw that she received a third-grade education, the most schools offered girls in this area, whose populace had a 95 percent illiteracy rate. Thereafter, Deledda received private lessons and undertook a program of self-education, reading Italian classics and romantic adventure novels. At fifteen she began publishing short fiction in the local newspaper and then in women's magazines. The publication of two novels, *Anime oneste* (Honest souls, 1895) and *La via del male* (The path of evil, 1896), earned Deledda immediate success among critics and general readers, who praised her innovative descriptions of Sardinia and the socioeconomic conditions and folklore shaping the lives of women and men in this region. She married and moved to Rome in 1900.

In both her life and literature Deledda devoted attention to women's issues.[14] She supported women's suffrage and divorce, and in 1908 participated with Maria Montessori in the opening ceremony of the first Congress of Italian Women in Rome. During her career Deledda wrote over 30 novels (10 of which were published during Fascism), and some 250 short stories, published in the daily press, literary journals, and women's publications. The international stature Deledda achieved, winning the Nobel Prize for Literature in 1926, had important implications for other Italian women writers. Speaking of Deledda's success, Guglielminetti stated: "Honorable men, think for a moment about the fact that this creature who is making our value emerge from the shadows, this creature of genius, is a woman."[15] After two operations, Deledda died of breast cancer in 1936.

Among the most striking aspects of Negri's literary growth is how closely she drew upon her own life's experience and knowledge to elaborate a socially committed form of writing that, in her words, would be "direct and cutting like the blade of a knife . . . and would voice the suffering and misery of the poor." (Croce, "Ada Negri," 351) Born in 1870, Negri became a rural schoolteacher and began to publish verses in a local newspaper at eighteen. The success of her first collection of poetry, (*Fatalità* 1892, trans. *Fate* 1906), was based largely on her frank, emotionally gripping portraits of people of the lower classes who, like her mother, eked out a living in a climate of social and economic injustice. Popular readers called Negri "the daughter of the people" while critics acclaimed her as an "antiliterary" social female poet. The autobiographic element is equally evident in Negri's subsequent writing. During her disastrous marriage to an industrialist, from whom she later separated, Negri wrote *Maternità*, (Motherhood, 1904), a collection of poems inspired by the births of her two daughters, the younger of whom died in infancy. After moving to Milan, Negri became active in groups for the defense of working women. In her collection *Le solitarie* (Solitary women, 1917) Negri composed fictional portraits of women she had met or encountered—clerks, shopkeepers, factory workers, servants, secretaries, and alienated wives and mothers—whose intellectual and creative abilities had no avenue of expression in society. This writer's ongoing concern with women's struggles in daily life shaped the content and form of her autobiographic work *Stella mattutina*, written shortly after her mother's death, and the short stories she contributed to the cultural page of the *Corriere della sera*, many of which were later published in collections. In 1931, one of four Mussolini awards, given by the Academy of Italy and instituted by the *Corriere della sera*, was conferred on Negri, and in 1940 she was the first woman to become a member of the Academy of Italy, a distinction that has likely forestalled serious consideration of her vast literary production. After experiencing the heavy bombing of Milan during the Second World War, Negri died on January 11, 1945.

Turin, an important cultural, economic, and political center, was the birthplace of both Prosperi (1883–?) and Guglielminetti (1881–1941). Although each received favorable reviews from discerning critics of their time, these women's lives and writings could hardly be more different. After earning a teaching certificate, Prosperi began to publish didactic fables and stories. Yet her first novel, *La paura di amare* (The fear of loving, 1911), was a notable critical success and received the Rovetta Literary Prize. An exceptionally prolific writer, Prosperi had published some thirty novels and short story collections by the late 1950s. During the years of Fascism, critics applauded her manner of analyzing the subtle alienation of private life through realistic portrayals of the lower middle class in squalid provincial and urban settings. Like Negri, Prosperi frequently uses spatial and domestic imagery to convey oppressive material conditions and social institutions that consume women's mental, emotional, and physical energies, as illustrated in "Beyond the Labyrinth."

Notably controversial for the way she lived and the literature she wrote, Guglielminetti won fame as a poet primarily with the publication of *Le vergini folli* (Foolish virgins, 1907) and *Le seduzioni* (Seductions, 1909). Although interest in her intimate relationship with the poet Guido Gozzano has overshadowed Guglielminetti's own literary achievements, in 1921 the respected critic G. A. Borgese compared her to a modern Sappho, possessing a remarkable "precision of imagination and expression."[16] Borgese also noted the innovative quality of her images of femininity, having a "harsh and masculine and rough" air about them, which disturbed the conservative male literary establishment. "Sensitivity" provides a typical example of how Guglielminetti's different female models challenged traditional gender roles. Like most women writers, Guglielminetti generated a popular following during the twenties and thirties, largely through her novels and short fiction, which focus on conflicts in sexual relations among the middle and upper classes. Guglielminetti's career was cut short when she died at age fifty-six from injuries sustained in a fall during an air-raid warning.

For their critical concern with avant-garde theories of literature circulating in Europe during the twenties and thirties, Astaldi (1900–?) and Manzini (1896–1974) represent a different dimension of Italian women's writing. Born in Udine, located in the northeastern corner of Italy, Astaldi received her degree in Literature and, by the 1940s was Professor of English Language and Literature at the University of Rome. Her work as literary critic in a predominantly male establishment is equally notable. In 1939 she published *Nascita e vicende del romanzo italiano* (The birth and development of the Italian novel). By the 1970s she had to her credit nine book-length critical studies on Italian and English writers, as well as five works of fiction and travel pieces, published in the thirties and forties. During the years of Fascism, Astaldi contributed to women's publications and the daily press. In her short fiction, Astaldi dramatizes conflicts of gender and generation, frequently deploying irony to critique the conservative ideas, attitudes, and expectations society brings to bear upon women.

Manzini, whose use of stream of consciousness and constant experimentation with language's limits and possibilities have led several critics to compare her to Virginia Woolf, was born in Pistoia, in Tuscany. She earned her degree in Literature at the University of Florence, and actively participated in critical debates conducted in the literary circle that formed around *Solaria*, an avant-garde Florentine journal. Manzini's first novel, *Tempo innamorato* (Time in love, 1928), and the short stories she published in the press during Fascism exhibit many traits that characterize her later narratives. Perhaps most striking is how Manzini uses imagery to render daily reality almost exclusively in terms of the characters' inner experiences of objects, sensations, memories, and fantasy.[17] This technique is particularly evident in "A White Cloud" and "The Pomegranate." Critics have consistently applauded Manzini's fictional works, awarding her some of the most prestigious literary prizes, including the Viareggio in 1956 for *La Sparviera* (The sparrow hawk), the Marzotto in 1961 for *Un'altra cosa* (Something else), and the Campiello in 1971 for *Ritratto in piedi* (Standing portrait), a novel about the author's father.

Maddalena Crispolti, Marinella Lodi, and Pia Rimini are among the many women who wrote for newspapers during Fascism, yet are entirely absent from literary histories and anthologies. The short stories republished in this volume exemplify these popular writers' tendency to employ techniques of realism and melodrama, thus creating detailed visual portraits of women's spaces within and outside the domestic walls, while heightening the dramatic power of daily conflicts. The many stories Rimini contributed to *Il giornale d'Italia* and *La stampa* focus on issues of gender and class, voicing strong social criticism of the economic, social, and cultural conditions marginalizing women. While "A Boy" dramatizes the ties of maternal self-sacrifice binding women of all classes, Rimini's other fiction gives particularly compassionate attention to the plight of women working for meager subsistence as field hands, tavern waitresses, laundresses, and maids, even investigating such issues as surrogate motherhood and prostitution, taboo subjects in the regime. Rimini is also the author of the novels *Pubertà* (Puberty, 1928) and *Eva ed il paracadute* (Eva and the parachute, 1931). While Rimini's narratives are generally studies of female oppression, those by Lodi, the most obscure among these writers, convey an awareness of autonomy and self-determination as desirable female values, achieved through personal choices. As in "Man and Death," her protagonists are frequently young women, in rural and urban settings, who reject the male ideal of romantic love to protect their independence. For instance, in "The Good Pilot" (1926), another excellent story, a middle-class working woman chooses not to follow her lover, but to pursue a future that is "gray but spacious, without any boundaries." Lodi also wrote the novel *Terra d'approdo* (The landing point, 1929). In a manner resembling Manzini's, Crispolti employs imagery to represent the rim of consciousness, exploring the contradictions between what is perceived, intuited, or repressed in women's lives. Like "A Drama in Silence," such stories as "The Mirror" (1931), "The Model" (1936), and "House Under Demolition" (1936) contrast women's different desires with the cultural ideal of femininity, whose repressiveness is conveyed through domestic imagery—picture frames, windows, mirrors, makeup, and clothing.

Like the vast majority of women's works published during Fascism, the short stories contributed to the cultural page developed female protagonists and revealed the specific dimensions of different female life erased within the Fascist cultural model of the "New Woman." The intimate nature of women's subjects and the personal position from which they speak posit a different notion of writing, accompanied by endeavors to craft new expressive forms. Guglielminetti, Negri, Prosperi, and Tartufari adapt literary language to the words and forms of everyday speech.[18] Moreover, the diverse images of femininity women create in such stories as "Man and Death," "Sensitivity," and "Woman with a Little Girl" differ markedly from those in fiction by such critically acclaimed male authors as Luigi Pirandello and Alberto Moravia, or by the popular writer Lucio D'Ambra, who each contributed short stories to the cultural page during Fascism. With little variation, misogynous attitudes pervade these writers' characterizations of the female as temptress, wife, or mother.[19] And, like the majority of male figures among the literary elite, Pirandello and Moravia tended to investigate the metaphysical and existential problems of man in Italian society.

The stories chosen for this collection represent differences in thought and style among women writers whose fiction on the cultural page became a staple form of entertainment in Italy during Fascism, anticipated and enjoyed by thousands of readers. I have included three stories each by Deledda, Manzini, and Negri because these writers were especially important in the literary community and on the cultural page of the dailies publishing their fiction.[20] With the exception of "Grace" by Deledda, which raises issues pertaining to women and writing and thus provides a critical context for the following narratives, the stories are arranged according to phases in the female life-course, from childhood to old age. This manner of organization was suggested by my reading of women's texts and of writings by Fascist exponents of their time. This arrangement also establishes thematic groupings, since issues related to socialization are more closely associated with childhood and adolescence, whereas concerns and possibilities of marriage, motherhood, and different female social roles are more typical of adulthood. The stories about aged women examine topics of increasing interest today; for example, female aging and the body, identity, and creativity. The different ways these female writers envision phases of women's lives provide a revealing contrast to the rigidly defined identity and roles of young girls and women as represented in Fascist speeches, articles, and propaganda, where they were addressed almost exclusively as the "Mothers," literal and figurative, of the nation.

In "Grace," a story inspired by an event in the author's life, Deledda alludes to the potentially subversive power of her writing. This first-person narrative, which tells a story within a story, offers unparalleled descriptions of the Sardinian landscape, folklore, and customs that ground both the narrator's drama and that experienced by a poor, aging woman and her son. While developing such themes as self-doubt, authority, social injustice, and vindication, Deledda articulates a notion of writing as a socially committed enterprise and creates a suggestive analogy between her role as author and the lentisk plant, which "hides the power of fire in its roots and oil for lamps and ointments in its wild fruit from all but the humble who know its secret." (24)

Similarly, the representations of female childhood and adolescence in "The Captain" and "Man and Death" critique established social relations of power, while undermining dominant notions of passivity, self-sacrifice, and conformity as desirable female values. Negri's story in particular invites discussion because of the way the author contrasts traits exhibited by the protagonist in childhood and adolescence. The indomitable five-year-old captain is an unforgettable character, whose actions and appearance—her hair the color of red bricks, eyes bright with phosphoric green flames, flaring nostrils, and set jaw—recast the traditional image of femininity. Yet the "dominating femininity" she embodies is threatened by economic and social conditions, "the same wheel that turns for so many poor young girls, and it only stops the day when you're no longer anyone at all." (31) While a sense of loss pervades Negri's story, Lodi creates an inspiring image of female self-determination through the first-person perceptions of a female adolescent in a rural community with rigidly defined gender roles: The boys wear pants and go out to work while the women wear skirts and stay home to dust. In this deceptively simple narrative the author examines complex ideas and conflicts provoked by the protagonist's changing awareness of self, and male authority, against which she rebels.

The majority of women's short stories in this collection, and on the cultural page, focus on female adult life, in many instances portraying contradictions between woman as ideal image and different forms of female identity, desire, and self-expression. Guglielminetti's rewriting of the Ariadne myth in "Sensitivity" critiques the objectification of women in society while recasting the terms of female desire. Arianna, who wishes to be valued for her intelligence and spiritual qualities, breaks three engagements with men whose vision is bound to her physical beauty, "a varnish destined to decay and disappear." (39) Although the character marries, her subversive power is not contained. Guglielminetti's sardonic closing line, which reveals that the object of Arianna's desire is blind, attests to her refusal to be defined by normative male vision. In "Beyond the Labyrinth," Prosperi's account of a young, successful bookkeeper's journey to confront her parents sets values deriving from female experience and ideals against those of male authority and power organizing the institutions of marriage and family. Pressured by her fiancé, Adriano, into demanding material compensation for her "illegitimate" birth, Leila meets with her mother and father. But these encounters allow Leila to see her parents with her own eyes and to reject the ideas she had internalized about herself and her relationship with Adriano. She turns him away. In "Fog," which may be read as a retelling of the St. Catherine story, Astaldi focuses on how marriage as a social ideal represses other meaningful forms of female self-expression, perhaps causing madness and death. Industrious and rich, like the Lombard plains where the story is set, Miss Lucia's life is dedicated not to male expectations, but to teaching and to cultivating her abundant, exotic garden. When she attempts to fashion herself into a prospective bride, however, she becomes a shadow of her self, "a ghost in the fog."

Various experiences of motherhood represented in these stories compete with the monolithic model of the exemplary Fascist "Mother." Through the transformation of domestic space and furnishings into symbols of women's literal and figurative confinement in "A Boy," Rimini analyzes a widow's profound alienation from self produced by the ideal of maternal self-sacrifice. This story is especially interesting for the way the author depicts the male child as an agent of oppression rather than a symbol of renewal. The motifs of entrapment and escape recur in Deledda's story, "Portrait of a Country Woman." Although the matriarch Annalena Bilsini embodies qualities generally associated with the Mother as a symbol of unity, possessing strength of character, body, and spirit, the woman's well-being is threatened by her repressed desire, which Deledda projects onto the landscape: "The large river, the luminous expanse of water and horizon, and the woodlands stretching back from the riverbanks had made her feel a sense of amazement and the desire that one of the pontoons . . . would break away and carry her and her buggy down the river, far away, to unknown lands." (71) Perhaps the most provocative expression of bodily, sensorial, and affective experiences of motherhood, Manzini's story, "The Pomegranate," invents new terms for mothering. Amidst elderly family members' urgings that Amalia exert the power her role as mother affords, the woman relives and reflects upon a web of memories and emotions shaping the relationship she has with her son. From Amalia's own understanding, the pomegranate emerges as a new metaphor for the relation between mother and child, symbolizing the possible coexistence of difference and unity, of autonomy and connection.

The last four selections speak of complex emotional, physical, and social aspects of female aging, which male texts of the twenties and thirties tended to ignore or to repress in the image of the aged woman as a unifying symbol of sage tranquility. This idealized image is forcefully critiqued by Crispolti in "A Drama in Silence." Narrated from the son's point of view, this story exposes contradictions between how he perceives his dead mother—"a shining beacon of maternal love"—and realities of the woman's life that threaten the image he venerated. The imagery associated with the mother—veils, clouds, shadows, and covers—bears special note for how it conveys the social ambivalence toward female sexuality in general and moreover toward that of women beyond the childbearing years. Negri's reflections on female aging in "Woman with a Little Girl," written when the writer was herself experiencing changes of old age, begin with a commonplace situation. As two women visit, a photograph of an older woman and a young girl catches the narrator's eye. Left alone to her thoughts, the narrator contemplates the images, interpreting the stories told by the aging woman's appearance. She sees neither fulfillment nor resignation, but questions without answers, and the unreconciled stirrings of suffering and affection, disillusionment and desire, youthfulness and decline. Also significant is the sense of a female collective Negri conveys through the narrator's identification with the older woman, the parallel history structuring the story, and the explicit address to female readers in the conclusion. While other stories provide partial visions of critical moments or conditions in women's life-course, from which we may infer a character's past or future, "A Life Story?" by Tartufari dramatizes a woman's experience of time and history as it changes throughout her lifetime. Like "Grace," this narrative is built inside another. While the narrator and her friend look at a family album, a photograph of the friend's dead mother, whose name momentarily slips the daughter's mind, inspires the narrator to tell a story about how the woman's life might have been. Tartufari ingeniously weaves the momentous events of popes and kings in nineteenth-century Italy into the texture of daily living, as Fabiola grows up in Rome, discovers the exciting possibilities of womanhood and courtship as well as the pangs of morning sickness, nursing her newborn, and tending to her children until they are grown. Tartufari's technique creates a complex portrayal of women's relation to history and to the books recording it, which are, she states, "the result of our fathers' politics."

The many short stories female authors published on the cultural page chronicle an important chapter in women's contribution to Italian life and culture during Fascism. We should not underestimate the social and symbolic importance these stories of female self-representation may have assumed among modern readers who had achieved or aspired to greater socioeconomic mobility. Although writings by Fascist propagandists addressed women as objects, attempting to engineer conformity with traditional feminine roles, short stories by female authors addressed women as subjects, and designed new possibilities for identification with nontraditional gender roles. The success of women's fiction published on the cultural page suggests that their stories addressed the concerns, interests, and tastes of a mass reading public, of which women were among the most avid readers.[21]

While the stories collected in this volume convey the authors' opposition to restrictive gender roles prescribed by Fascism, women of different classes, political parties, and religious ideas undertook a variety of activities as part of the Resistance movement. Acting independently or as part of organized networks, women supplied food, clothing, and hiding places to Jews and partisans, as well as Italian and foreign soldiers hunted by Fascist and Nazi authorities. Among other clandestine acts, women fought in partisan units and aided them by delivering messages and weapons, organized strikes, and sabotaged munitions and military supply factories. The mission these women conducted was twofold: They fought to liberate Italy from the Fascists and Nazis and to achieve their own emancipation, as clearly stated in the name of the Resistance organization formed by women in Turin in 1943, *Gruppi di difesa della donna e per l'assistenza ai combattenti per la libertà* (Groups for the defense of women and for the aid of the Freedom Fighters). Signaling female accomplishments on both fronts, women obtained the vote in 1945.

Although Deledda, Guglielminetti, and Negri died before Italian partisans and allied troops liberated the Italian peninsula from Fascism in the spring of 1945, Manzini and Prosperi—joined by such writers as Laudomia Bonanni, Alba De Céspedes, Natalia Ginzburg, and Anna Maria Ortese—played a major role in the project of social and artistic renewal undertaken on the cultural page during the postwar period. Their short stories tend to explore the lives of ordinary women for whom liberation from a repressive regime did not ameliorate the socially and psychologically oppressive dynamics of male-female relations. The uncanonized works in this volume have considerable historical and literary value for contemporary readers. As stories of female self-representation, they constitute an unparalleled perspective of women during Fascism, which displaces the cultural myths of romantic love, the mother, femininity, and virility that are the bases of conventional historical accounts. The innovations of theme, style, and narrative voice in women's writing propose new criteria for assessing their literary project and for revising the canon. Moreover, the endeavors of these women authors, not to define the female, but to analyze different identities and the means of their containment or expression in society, created memorable characters whose thoughts, desires, and ambitions sustain our reading interest and pleasure.

Notes

1. Giuliana Morandini's *La voce che è in lei: Antologia della narrativa femminile italiana tra '800 e '900* (Milano: Bompiani, 1980) is among the few anthologies to include works by these writers.

2. In the Afterword I examine other reasons why this period of Italian women's writing has been written out of literary history. Contributing factors include complex problems of postwar critical debate, periodization, and an unfamiliarity with the rich variety of poetry, novels, and short stories female authors published during the dictatorship.

3. See Alexander De Grand, *Italian Fascism: Its Origins and Development*, 2nd ed., (Lincoln: University of Nebraska Press, 1982), 30. For other classic historical studies that examine Fascism as a movement and ideology in its complexity, see Renzo De Felice, *Interpretations of Fascism*, trans. Brenda Huff Everett (Cambridge: Harvard University Press, 1977); David Forgacs, ed., *Rethinking Italian Fascism: Capitalism, Populism and Culture* (London: Lawrence and Wishart, 1986); Jeffrey Schnapp and Barbara Spackman, eds.,

Stanford Italian Review 8 (1988): 1–2 Adrian Lyttelton, *The Seizure of Power: Fascism in Italy 1919–1929* (New York: Charles Scribner's Sons, 1973); and Edward R. Tannenbaum, *The Fascist Experience: Italian Society and Culture 1922–1945* (New York: Basic Books, 1972).

4. Victoria de Grazia's pioneering work *The Culture of Consent: Mass Organization of Leisure in Fascist Italy* (Cambridge: Cambridge University Press, 1981) examines how the regime utilized leisure time organizations to structure private life and engineer mass consent.

5. Though a substantive and growing body of research on women's practices of daily living during Fascism exists in Italian, relatively few studies are available to English readers. Alexander De Grand's "Women Under Italian Fascism," *The Historical Journal* 19 (4) (1976): 947–68 continues to be an important reference, while Lesley Caldwell's "Reproducers of the Nation: Women and the Family in Fascist Policy," *Rethinking Italian Fascism*, 110–41 is more illustrative of current trends in research on women in the Fascist dictatorship. Luisa Passerini's *Fascism in Popular Memory: The Cultural Experience of the Turin Working Class* (Cambridge: Cambridge University Press, 1987) is of particular importance for the author's attention to women's cultural resistances to Fascism in their daily lives, as indicated by women's traditions, attitudes toward self, family, birth control practices, and work. Rich with archival information, Victoria de Grazia's newly published *How Fascism Ruled Women: Italy, 1922–1945* (Berkeley: University of California Press, 1992) makes a groundbreaking contribution to the historical study of women's complex relations to Fascist ideas, programs, and policies. For a thoughtful account of the diverse ways Italian women participated in the Resistance movement see Maria de Blasio Wilhelm, *The Other Italy: The Italian Resistance in World War II* (New York: W. W. Norton & Company, 1988) and Lucia Chiavola Birnbaum, *Liberazione della donna: Feminism in Italy* (Middletown: Wesleyan University Press, 1986).

6. Piero Meldini's *Sposa e madre esemplare: Ideologia e politica della donna e della famiglia durante il fascismo* (Firenze: Guaraldi, 1975) includes a substantive critical examination of the Fascist ideology of woman and policies implemented to reconstruct this model during the twenties and thirties. It also provides an impressive selection of articles written by Fascist exponents and published primarily in Fascist journals.

7. See Ugo Ojetti, "Ada Negri," *Cose viste* (Milano: Treves, 1923–1939), 190.

8. According to the Ministry of Popular Culture's press orders collected in Francesco Flora, *Note di servizio* (Milano: Mondadori, 1945), few directives regarded women writers and their works. And, as Tannenbaum has noted in *The Fascist Experience*, it was not uncommon practice for newspapers to violate press orders (224).

9. See Michele Giocondi, *Lettori in camicia nera: Narrativa di successo*

nell'Italia fascista (Messina-Firenze: G. D'Anna, 1978). Giocondi defines as bestsellers those books that sold 50,000 or more copies from the time of publication to 1943.

10. The cultural, or third, page (terza pagina) was created in 1901 by Alberto Bergamini, the editor of the Roman daily *Il giornale d'Italia*. Bergamini conceived of the cultural page as a tool to diffuse the ideas of renowned authors, historians, scientists, philosophers, and art critics among the readership. Thus, functioning as a bridge between intellectuals and the general reading public, the third page featured a broad variety of selections on the arts, politics, and social issues, and published short fiction, serialized novels, and poetry as well. Within ten years, the cultural page of *Il giornale d'Italia* had become a prototype for newspapers throughout Italy, and continues to be a vital part of Italian journalism. In the mid-twenties when Mussolini implemented stringent controls on the press, the focus of the third page shifted to literature and the arts. More importantly, editors began to publish more short fiction by popular writers on the cultural page which, in turn, increased newspaper circulation.

11. As stated in letters to the author from editors of the *Resto del Carlino* (19 March 1984) and *Corriere della sera* (19 March 1984) newspapers, the short fiction on the cultural page originally replaced serialized novels, and provided entertainment for "popular readers lacking the means to buy novels."

12. Among female contributors of note who are not represented in this volume are Alba De Céspedes, Daisy Di Carpenetto, Maria Luisa Fiumi, Lina Pietravalle, and Elisa Zanella Sismondo.

13. Deledda's childhood in Nuoro is powerfully portrayed in her autobiographic novel *Cosima*, trans. Martha King, (New York: Italica Press, 1988).

14. More information on Deledda's political undertakings and opinions on women's suffrage and divorce may be found in Carolyn Balducci, *A Self-Made Woman: Biography of Nobel-Prize-Winner Grazia Deledda* (Boston: Houghton Mifflin, 1975), Neria De Giovanni, *L'ora di Lilith: Su Grazia Deledda e la letteratura femminile del secondo Novecento* (Roma: Ellemme, 1987), and Deledda's novel *After the Divorce*, trans. Susan Ashe, (London: Quartet Books, 1985).

15. In Marziano Guglielminetti, *Amalia: La rivincita della femmina* (Genova: Costa & Nolan, 1987), 151.

16. See Giuseppe Antonio Borgese's Introduction to *Le seduzioni e Le vergini folli* (Torino: S. Lattes, 1921).

17. This point has been made by M. Assunta Parsani and Neria De Giovanni in *Femminile a confronto, tre realtà della narrativa contemporanea: Alba De Céspedes, Fausta Cialente, Gianna Manzini* (Manduria-Bari-Roma: Lacaita, 1984). For a particularly acute analysis of Manzini's poetics, see Giovanna Miceli-Jeffries, "Gianna Manzini's Poetics of Verbal Visualization," *Con-*

temporary Women Writers in Italy: A Modern Renaissance, ed. Santo L. Aricò (Amherst: University of Massachusetts Press, 1990), 91–106.

18. It is also true that popular male writers—Lucio D'Ambra for instance—rejected "high" Italian literary language.

19. These authors' conventional representations of female characters are more indicative of culturally entrenched ideas and biases than political support for the dictatorship. Although Pirandello supported Fascism, Moravia was an anti–Fascist intellectual, later barred from publishing his work in newspapers, and forced into hiding. A notable exception to this trend in male literary texts is Elio Vittorini's *In Sicily,* in *A Vittorini Omnibus* (New York: New Directions, 1960).

20. Some important women writers who made only occasional contributions to the dailies under consideration have been omitted (for instance, Sibilla Aleramo, who published two personal essays in the *Corriere della sera,* and Alba De Céspedes, who contributed the short story "A Secret" to *Il giornale d'Italia*).

21. Antonio Gramsci, a key figure in European Marxist theory, has underscored the formative influence fiction published in the daily press had on readers in Italy during this period by articulating their ideas, emotions, tastes, and aspirations. He is also among the few to have described the reading habits of women among the newspaper readership, stating that in decisions regarding which newspaper to buy "women have a large say in the choice and insist on the 'nice interesting novel.' " See *Selections from Cultural Writings,* eds. David Forgacs and Geoffrey Nowell-Smith (London: Lawrence and Wishart, 1985), 207. The particular appeal women's aesthetic had for female readers is suggested by the writer and critic Irene Brin, who stated in 1940 that she preferred literature by women. See Elisabetta Mondello, *La nuova italiana: La donna nella stampa e nella cultura del ventennio* (Roma: Riuniti, 1987), 192.

Grace

Grazia Deledda

My first small literary successes, like some great successes, also brought deep disappointments.

My family prohibited me from writing, since my future was supposed to be quite different from the kind I dreamed about; it was supposed to be a future devoted entirely to home life, to household chores, bare reality, raising a large family.

So long as I wrote children's stories, no one bothered much. But when the love stories started—with nighttime rendezvous, kisses, and sweet, compromising words—the persecution became relentless, from all my family, and was backed up by outsiders, who were the most frightening and dangerous of all.

A well-bred girl can't write about these things unless she is writing for experience or as a private outlet; if she somehow does arouse the curiosity of the young men in the district, not one of them will think of asking her to marry him.

It has always been the same the whole world over.

But this wasn't what troubled me. The arrows that were aimed straight at me and that wounded me most deeply came from the local literary critics. I especially remember a long, anonymous letter, written on official paper—like a legal bill of indictment— which arrived with perfect cruelty one beautiful September morning, just as we were about to leave for a holiday in the country. The holiday would last nine days, at the church of the Madonna of Valverde, in that Valverde basin, so dear to me because it was the wild cradle where my first dreams of art and love were fostered.

We slept—if you could call it sleeping, since much of the night was spent outside, by the light of the fires, dancing to accordion music—in small lean-tos built against the outside walls of the church. During the day, our house was the green clearing with its small stream, with stones for chairs, and the shade of the trees for awnings.

I carried the anonymous letter with me, like a hair shirt meant to remind me, amid earthly joys, of the atonement to come. Like the mystical outlaw who, according to tradition, founded the Valverde church, I hid myself among the rocks and lentisk plants to reread the charges that tore my work to shreds, as if it were that of a criminal.

The indictment's most precise and relentless blows were aimed at errors of grammar. But this wasn't what caused me the most pain; the pain that was killing me was seeing my poor creatures torn to shreds and trampled. Not even one survived the slaughter, and I was there with them, the most mistreated and broken.

And the tragic nature of my misfortune took on yet darker tones due to the fact that the letter, it was said, had been written by a woman.

But, as it happened, another woman soon did me justice.

As in those dreams that erase time and distance, but are bathed in the light of mysterious anguish that illuminates dreams, making the drowsy soul aware of the futility of the vision, I can see myself again perched on the ridge overlooking the stony valley, not far from some hollowed-out rocks, with low openings too small to enter. They are the *domus de janas*, famous megalithic monuments, prehistoric dwellings or tombs, where, as local legend has it, live little fairies—generous or evil, as the case may be.

The sky to the west, above the valley's far side, is deep crimson, and against this reflection the lentisk leaves look like a multitude of little flames.

Like an exile who gazes at the horizon, thinking about his lost country, I sit on a boulder and think that my literary career is obviously finished. My life is now like that solitary valley, without roads, without gardens, beneath a passionate light that will not be released except in the darkness of death.

I too will be like the lentisk, which hides the power of fire in its roots, and oil for lamps and ointments in its wild fruit from all but the humble who know its secret.

But it's not enough to live only for the poor, when you're sixteen years old, and believe you have the right to be in the sun, not planted on the ground.

It's injustice itself that weighs upon the poor; the injustice that, while helping a great man already at the pinnacle of human knowledge rise still higher, knocks down people with no education.

"Injustice . . . "

A voice has answered my thoughts, as if it were a mysterious echo within me. But no. The voice really belongs to someone else. Almost frightened, I turn around and see a tiny, old woman all dressed in black standing behind me, looking like one of the *janas* that live in the rock houses. Even her rosary is black. But two radiant objects brighten her appearance: a large, silver filigree medal with two sapphires, which hangs from the rosary, and her small face, which resembles the medal. Time has worn her face and the medal alike, leaving them with the same bright splendor. The old woman's eyes seem to have gotten their clear blue sparkle from looking at the two antique sapphires.

Now, her eyes are fixed upon me, and seem to have a new light, a sheen overlying the brilliance that was there before: the light of faith.

The old woman sits down on the ground, by my feet. Running her fingers over her rosary beads, as if she were kneeling before the Madonna of Valverde, she begins to tell me her request.

"It's because of injustice that I had to find you, my dear girl. I came here to talk with you, because over there, where everybody is staying, too many spiteful people could overhear us. Why are you looking at me like that? Don't you know who I am?"

Yes, now I recognize her. She's the little old woman who brought along a basket with everything she would need for sleeping and eating—the most important thing of all, the coffeepot. She passes the nine days of the celebration in a corner of the small room we were given to cook our meals.

She continued: "They say you know how to write better than lawyers do. Even the Queen reads your writing. It's a gift that God has given to you, and you must use it to help the poor. I need you to write a petition for me. I'll buy the paper needed for a legal document, even if it costs one lira. Will you do me this favor?"

"What is the petition for?"

She looked at me, surprised that I alone was unaware of her troubles.

"What? You don't know about it? My son, Sebastiano, my only child, was wrongly condemned to twenty years of prison, for a crime he didn't commit."

Stories like this always begin the same way, so I replied, "Everyone says that . . . "

But the little mother's face clouded over in an expression of such anguish that it upset me too.

"When I'm the one who tells you that Sebastiano is innocent, you have to believe me. And if you don't, what good is your talent?"

At first, I was flattered by her remark, then it made me think, it's true, lofty intelligence can penetrate and reveal the mystery of human events better than a serious judicial inquiry, however conscientious.

So I let the little old woman tell the long and complicated story of her Sebastiano. The beginning of the tragic story dated all the way back to his childhood and a tame hare he'd stolen from the pen next to his father's.

The owner of the hare, who was also a young boy, the only child of the herdsman living next to them, had sworn he would get even. Many years went by and Sebastiano, already a man of thirty, became engaged and was to be married. But the night before the wedding, the bride-to-be announced that she wasn't going to keep her promise to marry him.

No one ever found out why. It was said that someone had given her a drink of the *water of oblivion*, which made her forget her love for Sebastiano, and she wouldn't marry a man she didn't love.

Sebastiano resigned himself to her repeated refusals. After all, there are plenty of girls to marry in all corners of the world, and they'll jump out at the shake of a stick.

But then something horrible happened. One night, in the pen belonging to the girl's father, who was a herdsman too, ten cows were hamstrung while he was away. Since the hired hand watching over the herd resisted and cried out, he was stabbed to death.

"That night," the little mother insists, "my Sebastiano was sleeping at home by the fireside. Well, at dawn's light, he and I both heard a strange cry, piercing the walls around our house like the tip of a dagger. It was the scream of our neighbor from the adjoining fold—the hare's owner. Had he taken advantage of the situation, making it look like my son was guilty to get his revenge? We never knew for sure, except in our hearts. The fact is, Sebastiano was taken away and found guilty. And that night he had slept by the fireside, innocent as the fire itself."

Whether it was real or imagined, I didn't try to check the mother's version of what happened. Nor did I have any way to do so. It was as if I really were a lawyer, who, just to have a compelling case, accepts it on good faith, giving himself over completely to the side that can win him success. I wanted this success, so that I could redeem myself, most of all, in my own eyes.

"We'll write the petition. But whom should we write it to?"

"You're asking me, dear girl? To the Queen, of course." The sweet old woman said this as if I were about to write a private letter to a close aunt of mine, or maybe to my mother. Meanwhile, the name of the great, radiant Queen, shining high above our hearts like the morning star, sent shivers through my soul.

And I was caught in the circle of faith and fantasy of the little woman who blindly believed in the magical power of the written word, a power nonetheless that can truly span centuries and infinite spaces, and reach from the beggar to the king, if it springs from the pure of heart. So with the written word I'll speak to our Queen. Through my silent voice she will hear the little mother's heart speak, and justice will be done.

If only I had the petition here in front of me! With its innocent breath of humanity, it would take the place of all these insignificant pages that seem as if they were a story, yet aren't one. Or perhaps the petition was a literary document transformed and revived by deeply stirred memory to live a fuller life?

It's impossible to say. I know that it was written in beautiful handwriting, in the mother's name, and signed with her mark—a small shaky cross, a meaningful image of the mother herself, of her faith, of her pain.

I also wrote the address:

To Her Majesty
Margherita of Savoia
Queen of Italy
        Rome

Time went by, and there was no news.

The mother always kept hoping. I didn't think about it any more, happy that I had regained my self-confidence.

One day Sebastiano, who still had three years to serve, was set free by an amnesty. His mother came to see me, beaming as she had that day among the red lentisk plants of Valverde.

"See! The Queen granted the petition for mercy!"

I tried to tell her otherwise, but without any success. If the Queen hadn't spoken, she kept insisting, the amnesty decree wouldn't have set Sebastiano free.

As a sign of gratitude she offered me a keepsake that I have to this day: a little traveling flask, made from a small squash finely adorned with figures all around it—a work of art, of patience, of waiting, that the condemned man had made in prison.

Sole d'estate
1933

Grace 27

The Captain

Ada Negri

Whenever I left the house, I nearly always saw her just as I turned the corner onto the short, wide avenue leading up to the square where the streetcars ran by. Usually I would find her there on the sidewalk, whether the sun was shining or the clouds threatened to burst—in snow and wind, in hot weather and cold. She didn't go very far from her front door, surely because her mother had told her not to. She must have been the daughter of the concierge, or of a woman who lived on the first floor.

The first year I knew her, she couldn't have been more than five years old. She was the smallest in the group of kids she played with. Perhaps one of the boys was her brother; I don't know. She was the youngest, and often the only girl in a bunch of boys who would get back from school just dying to yell, raise a ruckus, roughhouse, and throw themselves into the wildest games. But everyone obeyed her. You could tell at a glance. Not only that, but I think all of them were actually a bit afraid of her.

I had never before with my own eyes seen such a tough and determined little girl, whose face and actions displayed such a striking will to dominate. I'll begin by saying that she had a mop of frizzy red hair, in a brick-red shade streaked with crimson—a rare color, unattractive, yet powerfully vibrant. Each lock of hair curled and glinted with light; crowning the top of her head, rising up like a crest, was a pea green or deep blue ribbon, which her mother had capriciously tied. On her small freckled face, her upturned nose and wide, dark nostrils, her flushed, high cheekbones and full lips formed a vision of coarse beauty, making her appear more mature than her age. Her upturned nose reminded me of a saying I'd heard from my mother a thousand times: "A woman with her nose in the air is nasty as a brewing storm." I didn't believe she was a really good little girl, even when she was asleep. Maybe it was so she could work off some of her uncontrollable energy that her mother left her outside so often to rough it out with the boys who were bigger than she was.

In the afternoon, the happy gang played all sorts of free-spirited and noisy games on that out-of-the way street. Cars and carriages rarely came by, and there weren't even many people. Not that it mattered much, since those little devils always knew exactly how to protect themselves from the cars, and other vehicles too. They dodged out of the way in the nick of time, as dogs do, instinctively calculating just how far they needed to move. There wasn't a chance they would be a hair off. When it suited them, the kids freely used the sidewalk and wide dirt strip between two rows of young plane-trees, where cars couldn't go. On the slabs of sidewalk they drew lines with chalk and in between them, made some cabalistic figures. They competed to see who was the best at jumping and flipping buttons the farthest. They got bocce ball games going that were as noisy as street fights, with hard balls made of compact rubber or wood. One of the children brought along a worn-out, crushed soccer ball—from who knows where—and they all fought over it. On days when it had rained and there was nothing else to do, the soft mud and mortar were perfect for building small caves, canals, and bridges. The little captain (which is what I called her to myself) seized the leadership of every game. She knew how to rule with an iron hand. One day I saw her arguing with a rascal twice her height. What a show! She raised her clenched fists in front of the enemy of the moment, challenging him with her determined chin and aggressive mouth, her voice shrill with anger, and her small eyes, phosphoric green like the first, sharp flame that rises when a match is struck.

She would have won, there was no doubt about it. The boy stood in front of her, furious but awkward, threatening but unable to touch a hair on her head. He seemed bewitched by those two unwavering dark green flames.

One March afternoon, as breaks in the light rain showers unsheathed blades of sunshine, and one sprinkle after another gave way to gusting whirlwinds, I came across the gang of kids walking in single file, in a marching step—one two, one two—along the dirt strip between the plane-trees, already golden with buds. They aimed their reeds and sticks like rifles. It goes without saying that the captain was leading the formation to fire. She identified with her part so passionately that her cheeks were flushed, and her little face looked almost cruel in the sunlight. From time to time she turned around, gave a sharp command, and then off they all went. Those five or six blockheads marched behind her, happy to be her soldiers, her slaves. I'm convinced they would have followed her joyfully to the bottom of a ditch.

I never caught her alone, unless I went out when her followers were caged-in at school. All by herself she was different. A small, sheathed dagger. Sitting on a stone in front of her house, or on a small chair in the doorway, she kept her head bowed over her toys. She had two beat-up dolls without any hair—I had never seen dolls so tortured and in such a sorry state—a little cart with one of its wheels missing, and some scraps of ribbon all heaped together. She looked very busy rocking one of the dolls, or both of them together, or dressing them with those ribbons. But her features remained hard, scornful. If she lifted her head up to look at someone passing by, that crest of green or deep blue silk seemed more aggressive than ever, standing erect on her curls, in that shade of red as violent as a punch in the eye.

I asked her once what her name was and why she didn't go to kindergarten. She looked me up and down, astonished and indignant. She wouldn't even answer me, but continued to look me up and down. At first I was hurt by it, then I felt like laughing. I enjoyed imagining that maybe the only name she had was the one I had nicknamed her, the only name that suited her: the captain. And maybe her mother wasn't her real mother at all, but a good woman who had taken her in from someone who had to stay anonymously in the shadows, and maybe the story of her birth was a mystery, of the kind you read about in old adventure novels. And maybe, just as mysterious and romantic, the destiny that awaited her; bizarre events and bizarre love affairs, in which she would have a firm hand and strong advantage, as she now had in games with her playmates. She would reveal and assert a dominating femininity and an intelligent, bold force of will. Theater? Dance? The movies? Who knew. With that passion for power, that hair, those eyes, that small solid body that promised to grow as straight as an arrow, she would also become beautiful, beautiful in her own way, of course. But yes! Very beautiful!

I was far away from home for a while, traveling. I returned, but only to shuttle back and forth between my small apartment in the city and a house in the country that belonged to some friends of mine. My life was going in a new direction. I didn't see the "captain" with her overbearing mop of hair again, and I didn't think about her any more.

Four or five years went by. But a few days ago I saw her near the entrance to her apartment building. I don't know how I was able to recognize her in the proper young lady who was coming home from school, accompanied by a bareheaded, elderly woman. It was her and yet not her. I could only tell who she was by her profile and her cheekbones, and by a hard expression of her mouth that still looked just the same. Everything else about her had changed or disappeared.

She was carrying a stack of books tightly under her arm. Slender, tall for her age, but with slightly broad shoulders, she looked awkward in her brown overcoat, her hair imprisoned in a beret that fit tightly over her head, leaving her high forehead bare. Her freckles stood out more on her pale, withdrawn face; her eyes stared at some vague spot, indifferent and distracted.

Her yet not her.

Older, bridled, weakened, her beauty spoiled, with her real first and last name written in rounded handwriting on the first page of her school notebooks and in her teacher's grade-book. I imagined her seated at her desk in classroom B or classroom C—the fourth or fifth grade—sitting quietly with her arms folded, her face blank as she listened to a grammar lesson. Then at home in the evening, bent over the dining room table, as she silently racked her brain over a division problem with decimals that wouldn't come out right.

Commanding the rowdy kids' maneuvers on the street? Never in my wildest dreams. And what of her need to dominate, her inborn magnetism that had led me to imagine her becoming an actress, a dancer, a movie star? Nonsense! Out of the question!

In a few years, a diploma from a technical school, a shorthand and typing course, a little French, an entry-level job, the ladder of promotions, a half-hearted love, and so on. The same old thing, the same wheel that turns for so many poor, young girls, and it only stops the day when you're no longer anyone at all. Everything grows dull, becomes deadened, and adapts to necessity.

Farewell, captain.

She didn't notice that I was watching her. Without turning around, she entered the doorway with the woman. My soul was left with a sense of bitterness, united with the image of an ordinary girl, going through that awkward stage of growing up that makes adolescent girls look like colorless, dry lizards. But the other image, the one of the small tyrant, the feared idol of her small world, didn't vanish. It stayed transparent in the background, unable to fade away, as sometimes happens when certain images are superimposed on the screen, at the movies.

Corriere della sera
17 April 1931

The Captain   31

Man and Death

Marinella Lodi

I didn't go to school and went out very rarely. Instead I studied with a priest. I had hostile ideas about life, and I was a skinny young girl with dark skin, large eyes, and two big legs that seemed like they belonged to someone else.

I had very vague ideas about everything, but there were two things I knew absolutely nothing about—men and death.

I knew that the men I saw in the streets (few streets as there were in my town!) were different from women, because they wore pants instead of skirts, and because they went out to work while women stayed at home and dusted.

Actually, I had always vaguely imagined that the reverend who gave me lessons was female, like us.

I didn't think about love. Death, close up, had never touched me, and from a distance, other people's funeral wagons, prayers, and grief made me run away, almost frozen with fear. I couldn't imagine what a person's face would look like if drained of life. I was even unaware that at times a person's face could also be strangely aflame with something just as vague—desire.

Our house was on a ravine. I liked it there, and I spent the evenings out on our small terrace, watching the moon run across the sky, and the shimmering water in the stream rush down the valley far below, between two shadows shaped like large fans.

I dreamed of walking away, crossing the countryside on a starlit night, just like that, to go live all by myself, and always in different places.

The affection I had for my father and mother was more a feeling of respect than tenderness, and I thought that growing up meant precisely to break away from them and to break away from everything. I already had too much of life, and only wanted to lighten my burden, to set myself free. Maybe this was why I looked at my legs with comic desperation. They were the only part of my body that mattered to me. I would have liked to trade them for the legs of a stork, or for two fresh, flexible reeds so I could pass over the hills in just one sweep, like the needle of a compass.

One summer, one of my father's cousins came to town with her husband. She had been married only a short while, and we hadn't seen her for many years. I didn't remember her, and at first she really annoyed me because she always wanted me to come over to her house. Then I got used to her.

She was twelve years older than I was, but I soon felt a maternal kind of tolerance toward her. She asked me a thousand questions and never waited for me to answer, and had a restlessness about her that was hard to put up with. But I liked her blond hair and milky white arms, which she always kept bare. She wore a lot of perfume, and changed her clothes two or three times a day. She constantly asked me, "Now tell the truth, are you in love?"

I couldn't understand this obsession to keep asking me the same question after I had already answered *no*, in amazement, the first time. Yet she still wouldn't drop it. "But if you don't think about some man when you're thirteen, what do you think about? You must have some shadowy picture of a man, or at least hope to meet one. That's always on every girl's mind!"

Then I started to worry that I was incomplete, and thought I noticed something missing inside me where these shadowy dreams and hopes should be, according to what my cousin said.

Her husband was much older than she was. Tall and a bit slouchy, he had a hooked nose and frizzy hair that gleamed with pomade. She adored him though, and I'd heard that she had run away with him before they got married so that she wouldn't have to give in to her relatives, who were trying to make her marry a younger and richer man.

As she hugged him and put her head on his shoulder, she'd say to me, "Come on now! Don't you dream about having a handsome, sweet husband like him sometime soon?"

I'd look at her, but didn't have the courage to answer, because the immense joy she felt only made me sorry for her.

Old hooked-nose would nibble at her arms and say, looking at her and me with two bright little eyes, "You smell so good Maria! You smell like fruit!" I couldn't believe Maria would let him do that, and actually nestle her whole body against him like a hen. Then I'd pull my sleeves down, way down to my fingernails, sadly wishing the material would stretch even further. But I was sorry for feeling disgusted by this man, who was able to make a woman—my cousin—happy just the same.

He didn't ever talk to me alone, though. There was a distance between us, created by my own distrust and uneasiness around him and, perhaps, by his dislike for me. Of course I felt as if I were an imposition in his house, even though I went there reluctantly.

One time, as he and his wife talked to each other from different rooms, I heard him say, "That sulky girl always getting in the way? She's ugly!" It didn't hurt my feelings because I understood why he'd want to be alone with his wife, who was so beautiful, and so good that she even let an ugly, old man like him kiss her.

Another time, I heard him raise his voice during a hushed argument and declare, "What do you mean! She's cold and selfish!" This confused me.

They had her elderly father, who suffered from heart problems, living with them. He always stayed in the bedroom, sitting in an armchair and breathing heavily as he looked out the window with his empty eyes, as though peering out from two deep caves. He also called me over constantly to keep him company, but I was afraid to be alone in his room because it always seemed as if a third presence, something indefinable, was hovering in the air. I didn't dare say the word *death* even to myself, fearing I might evoke it, and I looked suspiciously at the curtains as they seemed to billow and move. . . .

In moments like those I even wished for my cousins and the boring sight of them caressing each other. Most of all, I thought about the day when they would all leave again, fooling myself into thinking I would go back to being peacefully unaware right away.

Then, one morning they ran to our house to tell us the old man had died. I didn't want to set foot in that house where the mysterious event had happened for anything in the world, but my mother made me go along with her because she thought we had to show our relatives how stricken we were with grief, to which I was immune. So long as I didn't have to go into the dead man's room, I agreed to cross the threshold of that house, but I trembled, not knowing what to expect. When I saw the sorrowful face on my cousin's husband though, I reproached myself, repeating those distant words: *cold, selfish*. But I couldn't change how terrified I felt deep inside.

"Try to calm Maria down a bit. She's in an awful state," he said to my mother, pointing to the nearest door, from which slivers of lamplight strained out. "She's in there. I can't take it anymore. She keeps fainting, and throws herself into my arms crying, 'I only have you now! You're all I have left!' It's as if she's afraid I won't be enough. . . . "

"Of course you're all she has! You have to show her how much you love her," answered my mother, thinking the woman's fears weren't all that absurd. Then she left me alone with him, and told him to keep me company.

I didn't know what to say to him. He was so serious and sad, I didn't dare speak to him. I was sorry I had disliked him so much, yet I disliked him even more now. I was afraid he would burst into tears, and the thought of having to comfort him really bothered me; my intense uneasiness made me think that he could faint in my arms too. What would I do with him? Luckily there was a large couch in the room that I thought could come in handy. But the door out was far away, down at the other end of the room. The door near by . . . So I wouldn't see the light glowing sadly from that door I went over to the window. He followed me without saying anything, and we looked outside together. He was sighing. I didn't feel any sympathy for him, and thought I was awful. "He's suffering," I said to myself, "and I'm only thinking about myself and how much I detest him!"

It was Sunday, and with the buzzing in the crowded, festive street, the darkness and silence behind us seemed even more mournful. Every now and then we heard a sob burst out in the other room behind us: Maria. As she began to cry, I'd cough and stamp my feet so he wouldn't hear her; I wished I was able to talk to him to distract him. Then it seemed like he was standing too close to me, and I moved so I wouldn't bother him. I kept getting the same impression until, between one sigh and another, I had nowhere to go but up against the wall, but I still felt his manly warmth and smell—so new to me, and repulsive—close by. Churning inside, I was torn between the strange uneasiness and the pity he made me feel.

But the painful astonishment I felt turned to indignation and fear when I was forced to realize that he was touching me deliberately. I trembled and blushed, ashamed of myself and of him; my only instinct was to move away, but I couldn't. I felt my eyes fill with tears for this assault on my emotions, but I didn't let even one fall, so I wouldn't have to accept what seemed to be happening. I couldn't admit that such a horrible thing was true. What did he want, what was he doing, and why, then, did he continue to sigh? I didn't dare look at him because I didn't know what I would now find in those eyes of his, eyes I'd never really looked into. I wanted to say "I'm hot," so I could free myself, but I was afraid he'd take it the *other* way from the sound of my voice, and then, strengthened by his authority as a relative, would accuse me of being immodest. I was the one being humiliated. I was suffering.

I leaned still further out the window so I would be less alone with him in the darkness—and less near to death. He was breathing heavily on my neck, like the old man when he was alive, and I thought he was the one behind me. Anyhow, I felt as if the unknown were breathing ardently on the nape of my neck. . . . To escape the reality of his cautious and insinuating hands I squashed myself against the windowsill and felt a deep pain in my chest; that was when I realized I had breasts. All of a sudden I thought my dresses were too short, my neck too bare, my legs too big; in a desperate race my hands followed his to push them away, to protect myself, to cover my body. . . .

It was no use! His hands were everywhere.

I said harshly, "Your wife is crying," thinking I would cruelly shake him back to his senses and deeply hurt his feelings. He didn't pay any attention to me, and besides, it wasn't true. There wasn't a sound coming from the dead man's room anymore. I was alone and in agony.

He was silently wrapping himself around me like an octopus; he gripped me from every side with his legs, his arms, his breath, and I felt myself disappear, absorbed by the wicked way he stuck to me. Finally his face was so close to my mouth that I could see . . .

Oh, in those feared and almost unknown eyes I saw only this: emptiness. But that made his face frightening, as a mysterious, moist ecstasy dripped from his idiotic smile. Then I heard a slurred voice mumble something like, "Such a young girl, and you're already a woman. My God!" I heard other, more distant words: "You smell like fruit, Maria!" And as if I were in a dream, with Maria's moaning in some other part of the house—all dark and icy like a tomb—the horror that living man made me feel was so strong I managed to wriggle free and throw myself quickly toward the closest door. I opened it . . .

The dead man was lying on the bed, on top of a damask blanket that was as green as a meadow. He was alone. His hands were crossed on his chest, now peacefully freed from the struggle to breathe, and he had a smile on his face; the disturbing circles around his eyes and mouth had disappeared. He inspired peacefulness and almost drew me to him. I quickly crossed the room and knelt down close to the low bed. I took his icy hands tightly in mine and rested my burning forehead against them, feeling the wild pounding in my temples fade against the perfect immobility of those hands.

I stayed like that, clinging tightly to the funereal blanket, under the protection of the four flickering candles as if I were in a place no one could violate, while in the living room next to me angry steps paced up and down in the darkness.

When I won back my solitude, I became peaceful again, but I was no longer unknowing, and I had ideas about life that were even more hostile and clear. I'd come to know man and death, and had immediately preferred the latter.

Il giornale d'Italia
12 July 1925

Sensitivity

Amalia Guglielminetti

Who knows what ever possessed them to give her the name Arianna*—so heavy to bear, like marble or a bronze statue.

The first time I saw her was in Venice, in Saint Mark's Square, as she, like everyone else, took part in the delightfully foolish scene that is perfect for taking pictures and makes foreigners go wild—throwing crumbs to the pigeons. All the wandering tourists had their cameras focused on her, as her young, dazzling beauty stood out among a flash of multicolored wings.

That autumn, as the warm sunshine lingered, turning the dour majesty of the doges' palaces golden and soft, Venice became fascinating in ways I'd never noticed before and kept me entranced on the banks of the green water. At first I stayed in a hotel on the Lido, and then moved to the Danieli, where I could more often enjoy a cinematic view of the Bridge of Sighs and a literary view of George Sand and Alfred De Musset, those almost legendary lovers.

Arianna lived at the Danieli too, with an older uncle who had a thick gray mustache. It wasn't clear what nationality he was, and he spoke every language except Italian. She had been born in Paris, but her mother had been pure Roman. Arianna seemed happy to talk with me and to explore Venice together. After a few days we became friends, and one evening she made a comment about her name, with a slight,

---

*In English, Ariadne, the name of the Greek goddess.—TRANS.

awkward smile on her face, "Arianna. It's a ridiculous name."

I looked at her, without smiling. She did have that true, classical beauty of immortal deities. An austere beauty—though softened by her youthful age of twentysome years—without any affectation and almost without any modern elegance, but possessing pure lines and enchanting grace.

"It's a name that only a beautiful woman can handle. And you are beautiful."

She seemed to frown, and in that moment the look on her face had the angry sadness of Medusa's.

"No, please don't! Not you too! Don't you start singing that same old tune! I'm twenty-three years old. For seven years all I've heard people say around me is: You're beautiful!"

I shook my head and laughed incredulously.

"Doesn't that make you happy at all? Any woman would like to be in your place. Montesquieu said . . . "

"Leave Montesquieu out of it. Being beautiful is the least of my qualities. It's only how I look on the outside, a varnish destined to decay and disappear with time. There's something inside me that's worth much more."

"What is it?"

She hesitated a few seconds, with her brow furrowed like a tempestuous goddess, then said in a low voice, "My soul, my intelligence, my sensitivity."

Since we were almost strangers, perhaps destined to never meet again, we confided in each other about many of those emotionally and spiritually painful things that people don't tell even to their childhood girlfriends, or most loyal friends.

Arianna told me she had been engaged three times, and each of those times had broken the nuptial chains as they were about to be riveted onto her wrists.

"You aren't suited for chains either," I observed with a little bitterness.

"On the contrary! I'd like the kind of undying, all-embracing love that would sweep me away, but love that wouldn't get pleasure only from how I look, and wouldn't be enraptured purely by the color of my eyes and the shape of my shoulders. Sometimes I feel as if I were a rare specimen for a zoo, who is asked nothing more than to show the visitors its beautiful fur and a contented muzzle."

"It's obvious that one of your fiancés was a painter."

"How did you know?"

"You're talking about shape and color."

"You're right. He was a Belgian painter. We were engaged for two and a half months, and he painted nineteen portraits of me: full face, profile, three quarters, four-fifths."

"But did you love him?"

"For a week, maybe. The love affair lasted a week, then the portraits started. When he began to paint the twentieth one, I caught a train and left for good, abruptly breaking all ties with him."

"You have more will power than I would have imagined. Tell me about your next fiancé. What was he? A sculptor?"

"No, he was a science professor, specialized in entomology. I wasn't much more important to him than one of his butterflies.

"One day I decided to penetrate the laboratory where my fiancé, the professor, worked, so I could study the fascinating mysteries of nature too, and learn how the flowers and stones and metals live, and how they love. . . . He said: 'Go away! You're too beautiful to take an interest in these things. Studies, learning, culture, science are only suitable for ugly women who don't have any other more pleasant ways to occupy their lives. Go away!' So I did go away, and never went back.

"It's not worth talking about my third fiancé. He was a middle-aged man of good Parisian society, who loved most of all to show me off in ballrooms or tearooms, or else seated beside him in his car at the Bois, or leaning against the railing of his box seats at the opera. I was an impressive ornament that he needed to spruce up the gilding of his rather tarnished armor. Nothing more."

Arianna turned silent and frowned, her face looking upset and full of sadness, like Medusa with curling snakes rising from her head.

We happened to see each other at Capri, two years later. Arianna was traveling with a female companion on the boat headed for the Blue Grotto. As she came toward me, she reached out for me, with her face full of a deep, contained joy that made her beauty more enigmatic and at the same time more human and more feminine.

The boat was full of Germans—dull, sluggish, solemn, but all the same they stealthily looked at her in almost dismayed stupefaction.

"I'm happy," she confided without smiling, as she squeezed my arm, her hand unusually nervous. "Six months ago I married the man I'd been looking years for, someone who loves me almost exclusively for my spiritual qualities, who feels joy in my intelligence, who enjoys my sensitivity, and doesn't think my intellectual curiosity is useless and disagreeable. We live off by ourselves, secluded in a small villa at Anacapri, that green, green hill you see over there, surrounded by vineyards and warmed by an almost African sunshine. Each day goes by for us like the last, delicious, in a passion that never ends."

She spoke with a slight exaltation that had the flavor of a story and of reality.

"Tell me about him, you adorable, absurd creature," I urged her on with slightly biting curiosity. "Hasn't your husband said that eternal refrain you detest yet, 'You're beautiful!'?"

"No."

"Did you tell him yourself not to say it?"

"No."

"Is he old? Is he slow-witted? Is he insensitive?"

"No. He's young. He's a disabled war veteran. He's blind."

Il giornale d'Italia
10 September 1933

Baptisms

Grazia Deledda

By God's will, after a long winter drought that had petrified the land and plants, there was finally a classic night of wind, driving rain, thunder, and lightning. The whole house shook, but with joy it seemed, harmonizing with its owner as he rubbed his hands, and answering the fields quivering outside as they became drunk with water.

"At last, hey, Mariù? What, are you sleeping already, with all this music going on?"

His wife had been in bed for quite a while, and she was curled up on her side of the mattress, trembling and happy like everyone else, but harboring a sense of fear deep in her soul. She was praying, and it was only when her husband's heavy, half-naked body, with its ruddy thighs and legs mottled with little black curly hairs, and with its big icy feet, made the mattress stubble crackle, that she opened her eyes, and the reflection in the window ablaze with lightning made it seem like her eyes were ablaze too. Then she pulled the covers up again, and her husband's voice reached her from far away, almost like an echo under the feather quilts. It was a mean voice—in fact, a willingly cruel one.

"I'm thinking, Mariù, about the people who are lost out in the fields, with no place to take cover, or traveling without even an umbrella. Hey, with that clear sky we had today, who could have guessed there would be a storm? At least there's no more chance of hail. It's raining cats and dogs now. It was about time."

His wife was praying, thanking God for his goodness. The man laughed, as if he were dreaming.

"Yes, there are people traveling out there in this foul weather. And we're here safe at home, in our own comfortable bed, with everything in its place, the livestock well taken care of, the field getting its strength back. We can't complain. As my father used to say: 'Things are bad, but they could be worse.' "

"So be it," whispered the woman.

"I'm happy for our little girl, too. What more could anyone want? A good marriage with a rich, strapping, honest man. And best of all, they don't live too close by. When people live too close to each other there's always so much friction, so many disagreements and misunderstandings. So, the two of them live over there, eight kilometers away, and we live here. We see each other on all the holidays, and this way they're really holidays for everyone. I know, you would have liked to keep your little girl tied to your apron strings your whole life—and her husband too! You women think everything is so easy, so simple. But life is hard."

"Life," he repeated in a loud voice, even though his wife didn't say a word, "is like everything else—like animals, plants, grass. You have to keep it in check, to trim it, to mow it. Or think of it like a beard. If you don't shave it every eight days, even though shaving's a nuisance and you risk cutting yourself, it invades your face and drives you away from the company of civilized men."

His wife doesn't answer. After so many years she's gotten used to the rough philosophy that her husband puts into practice everyday. She's thinking about her "little girl" instead, who is still, in her eyes, not only little, but actually a baby, born just a few days ago, mute, blind, shapeless, yet already beautiful, sensitive, vibrant with life.

To her it seems like the day of the baptism. The godmother is holding the newborn baby girl, all dressed in pink, and the priest pronounces the solemn words.

"I believe. I renounce."

"I believe. I renounce," answer the onlookers.

Only the tiny baby doesn't answer. In fact, she waves her fists with a strength that makes her mother smile; grimaces of protest, boredom, and disgust move across her little face as if a tempestuous dream were stirring her still-sleeping soul.

But the father keeps an eye on the mother as well as the daughter, and in the festive, gilt picture of the baptism, his coarse dominating figure, with his black eyes and black beard, and his eyebrows that look like a mustache, overpowers even the priest's.

That same frown reappeared on his face as he sat up in bed and through the storm's din heard someone knocking at the door.

His wife, already drowsy, didn't trouble herself over who it might, or might not, be. Maybe a neighbor who needed something right away; maybe one of those troublesome, unfortunate travelers her husband had been talking about before, people with no place to stay. Her husband would take care of it.

In fact, he had already jumped out of bed, and with a silence not usual for him, had lit the lamp and was getting dressed. He wasn't in much of a hurry either. Indeed, he got dressed with an almost ostentatious slowness, as if to give himself time to prepare an answer for the untimely visitor. But his heart was beating loudly, echoing the knocks at the door, and his fingers trembled as they searched for the buttons on his clothes. This silence of his, this hesitation, worried the woman. Shadows passed through her mind, and even her heart began a kind of whining. Her golden-silver head emerged from the pillows and covers as if it were rising from a foamy wave; her large blue eyes, like a frightened little girl's, searched in vain for those of her husband.

But he was already on his way out of the room, taking the lamp with him.

"Dear Lord," cried the woman, and she listened with all her might through the chaos of the storm, the bedcovers, and the turmoil of her heart.

Downstairs, the man must have opened the door because she couldn't hear any more knocking. He must have been talking something over with the untimely visitor at the door because he didn't come back upstairs.

The wife sat up, straining to hear, but only the noise of the storm grazed her ears, and it seemed as if the cold, dying rain penetrated clear to her heart.

A panicked sense of terror kept her from getting out of the bed. But then a scream rose from the road, shaking the room and lighting it up with the rumble and flash of lightning.

"Mama!"

The woman threw herself out of bed, and ran down the stairs to the doorway. In her nightgown, and all disheveled, she looked as if she were running from a fire. Her husband, pelted by rain, was standing at the barely open door and talking to someone he was keeping out. As soon as he realized that his wife was at his back, he swung around, livid, his face soaked as if with the sweat of battle, and opened the door some more, but kept blocking it with his brawny arms. And she saw the figure that her confused eyes had already imagined.

There was her daughter, pale and dripping with water like someone who had drowned, hopelessly asking to come in.

"Mama, mama . . . "

"My child, what have you done?"

The mother and daughter both tried to move the man, so they could hold each other, but he wouldn't budge. Now, in fact, he had regained his look of cruel mockery and seemed to be enjoying the struggle.

"Mama, mama! I ran away from home because he spoke harshly to me. I don't want to stay with him anymore. I want to come back home. I ran away, on foot, just like I was . . . "

The mother pressed her head against the man's neck as though she wanted to bite him, but she was crying.

"That's enough of this," he said then, "it's time to put an end to this scene! This young lady and I are going to take the bicycles and ride back to *her house*."

"At least let her come in to dry off."

"Absolutely not! Otherwise she'll make a habit of taking these little walks, and who knows where it will end? Come on, get me the bicycles and my coat. Hey, who do you think I'm talking to? Quit making faces! Look, the neighbors are turning on their lights."

"Mama, mama," whimpered the daughter, curling up on the doorstep, "let me come in, for the love of Christ. I'm not going back, no! I'll die, I'll kill myself!"

"Get us the bicycles, for God's sake, or tonight you'll both get a beating. Don't make me take my hands off this door!"

The two voices rang out together, as in a tragicomic duet, accompanied by the chorus of the storm.

"Mama, for the love of Christ . . . "

The woman passed her hand over her face, as if tearing off a veil. Once again, in a flash of lightning, she saw her little baby girl dressed in pink, sprinkled by the baptismal water.

"I believe. I renounce."

And she went to get first one bicycle, and then the other, and then her husband's coat. She also brought a shawl for her "little girl." But she wouldn't take it. Her little girl was already well covered by her shawl of rain and obedience to destiny.

As the bicycles got farther away, the fury of the rain and wind abated. Like a roaring crowd that grows quiet at the passing of a calming figure, the storm seemed to make way for those two people going through it by the force of their pain.

For the man also felt full of anguish deep inside—the anguish of a will that rises above every instinct to withdraw and rest.

But after they'd arrived at the newlyweds' home, and the two young people had made up, partly out of love, but mostly because they felt the inexorable power that already held them, the father, without wanting to, without even knowing it, felt himself close to the first great men who had used violence to create laws for their fellow human beings.

Corriere della sera
6 April 1926

Beyond the Labyrinth

Carola Prosperi

*T*he letter said: "Yes my dear, my beloved Leila, I feel more and more certain that the time has come to take the final step. We've been engaged way too long, for three years! It's been three years since I met you at the cotton mill where you work. It's too bad I wasn't able to be more successful in my job there, even with all of your influence and valuable support. But let's not dream about how the past might have been; let's think about the present. As you know, I have a good job here, a decent salary, and most importantly, the chance to move ahead. If you wanted to, you could keep your job, since the trip from the city to this little town doesn't cost hardly anything if you buy a pass. We could even get married right away, if, as you know, we had enough money to get started in a place of our own. Don't talk to me about your savings! They're almost nothing. I've never been able to put anything aside, and I can't ask my mother or sister for money. They're both widows living on just a small pension. You see, my dear Leila, the moment has absolutely come when you have to shake yourself out of your indifference and take a stand to fight for our love. Your mother owns a store that makes a profit, and your father is an elegant man who makes a good living. He goes to the theater and concerts with his wife and his other daughters. You have to go see your mother and father. Get them with their backs against the wall and remind them of their sacred duties. Then, if they don't want to give you anything, threaten them with the possibility that our engagement might be called off. After all,

they ought to think about how lucky it is that along the way you happened to meet a person like me. . . . "

Leila dropped the sheet of paper onto her small writing table. "A
person like me!" Adriano was always repeating that phrase. That was
why everyone ended up disliking him, even at the cotton mill. But people were unfair, and Adriano was always right. Leila got up and took
from the coat rack an old overcoat she wore at home when it was damp.
With her hands in her pockets, she started to pace up and down the
long, narrow room, which was crowded with furniture and junk; it
looked more like a living room done in the worst taste than a cozy
bedroom. She stopped in front of the window, which was high and
protected by an iron grating. Although her room was on the ground
floor, she could see only the tops of open umbrellas passing by, and
the yellow wall of the building across the way—the orphanage. Leila
thought bitterly about how, in Adriano's opinion, she should be pitied
more than those orphans in deep blue dresses, with white bonnets,
and little pale faces that she sometimes saw behind the windows. She
had been born twenty-four years earlier, the daughter of two careless
people who'd been in love. They were both very young and full of passion, and they lived near by each other in the country. The problem
was that their families, who were enemies, never allowed them to get
married. Then the fickle young man fell in love with someone else;
the young woman, tired of waiting, had a good opportunity to settle
down with someone . . . As for Leila, she spent her childhood with
a wetnurse, who cared for her a lot, then she went to live with an older
woman—the cousin of her maternal grandmother—who grumbled all
the time, but didn't treat her badly, and finally Leila went to a boarding school to study to get her diploma in bookkeeping. That was when
her father first came to see her. He spoke to her with great serious-
ness, promising her help and affection, so long as she realized just how
things stood and didn't compromise his position with his family.

To begin with, he got her the job at the cotton mill in a small town
on the plains, near the city. Intelligent, hard-working, and conscientious, Leila was, right from the start, admired, appreciated, and well
liked by everyone at the cotton mill. All that time she had never thought
of herself as an outcast, and hadn't been aware of being so unfortunate.
But when Adriano showed an interest in her, with his tender sighs and
his passionate way of looking at her, madrigals, and declarations of love,
she confided in him and told him about herself and her parents. Then,
when she was faced with his astonishment, his disdain, and his pity—
she felt humiliated and unhappy, oppressed by an unfair destiny and
full of resentment toward her careless parents. Adriano was right, she
needed to push their backs up against the wall. Let them pay, provide

for their daughter, and take care of their obligations to her. If not, she really would have to believe that those orphans in deep blue dresses and white bonnets, who prayed and worked inside that big yellow house facing her, were better off than she was.

She stared at the orphanage for a long time, and then went into the dining room to join the two elderly ladies who rented her the room. Everyone called them "the mayor's daughters" because ages ago their late father had been the town's mayor. Leila sat down at the table without saying a word, and all Miss Dele's and Miss Genia's coaxing to get her to say something was completely useless. "Old, stingy witches," Leila thought contemptuously, "like everything else around them—shabby, poor, tasteless! Their house is about as pleasant as a cave, and their tiny garden looks as cheerful as a well. And they think they own who knows what!" She felt disagreeable, rude, and shabby inside that house too, but it was impossible for her to make herself seem any better. She got up without saying a word, returned to her room, and went to bed. She had trouble getting to sleep, and tossed and turned all night. She finally fell into a deep sleep in the morning, just before Miss Dele timidly rapped on the door to wake her at the usual time, "Miss Leila!" She answered sharply, and got up grumbling. Then she stopped off at the cotton mill to quickly take care of a few things and to let them know she was running into the city on personal business. If only the weather had been good! But no, even from the window of the train the countryside looked gray, dull, deserted, and it was drizzling in the city. At that time of the morning her mother would already be at the store! At the thought that soon she would come face to face with that simple fact, Leila felt overcome by an indescribable uneasiness. I have to be strong. This was what Adriano meant by "taking a stand to fight for his love." I have to be strong.

Her mother was in the store, behind the counter, showing a lady some silk stockings, and passionately praising all their fine qualities. Seeing Leila come in, she blinked and winced slightly, and looked worried and afraid. Leila sat down in a corner to wait and nodded hello to an elderly saleswoman, who thought she was the owner's niece. She took a long look at the young girls working there, whispering to each other as they put some boxes in order. Then she took a hard look at her mother. Her hair needed to be combed; some strands were hanging loose around her thin cheeks, strands of black mixed with gray. And yet she wasn't old, forty-two or forty-three . . . She must not have slept well, and probably rushed out of the house without having breakfast; it was clear in her pale face, the bags under her eyes, and how exhausted she looked. And yet she talked on and on! She offered the customer all sorts of merchandise so tirelessly. She didn't let up even at the door; as she handed the woman the tiny package (just one pair of stockings), she continued fervently: "We have all kinds of woolen garments too, everything you might need for winter sports." Leila felt like going over to pull her away, to tell her, "But Mama, you bother people that way. That woman will never come back to your store. Why do you work so hard?"

Her mother stopped in front of her, sighed, and looked anxiously into her eyes. "Well now, Leila, everything's going okay with you, isn't it?" She sat beside her, on the edge of her chair, keeping an eye on the salesgirls to make sure they didn't take advantage of the situation and stand around doing nothing. Knowing Leila was alright made her feel better. As far as everything else was concerned, she was loaded with problems: Her husband had problems with his liver, her children at boarding school refused to study.

"But why," Leila said, "why don't you take better care of yourself? Look after your health, try to eat better." And she thought, "I could easily have bought her a box of chocolates. I have more money than I really need." She said loudly, "I'll bring you some pastries the next time. Do you like them?" A rush of emotion made her mother's eyes suddenly turn red with tears. "Oh, you're a kind girl, you're so kind."

"Don't be silly!" And Leila, who loathed emotional scenes, hurried to get out of there. "After all," she thought, as she headed for her father's office, "what fault was it of hers? He is the most to blame. He makes a lot of money, goes to the theater and concerts with his wife and daughters. He's the one I need to settle things with. If he doesn't see me right away, he'll hear about it!"

He saw her immediately. The offices were buzzing with work— telephones were ringing, typewriters were clacking away. Her father was in the main office, in charge of that world, and the people who went in to see him had a submissive look on their faces. But when he saw her come in, his own hard, determined face turned submissive and worried. It was clear that she was the one person in the world who could make that man afraid, that man whose face was still strong and youthful under his silver hair.

"Oh, my dear Leila, what a surprise. . . . " She sat down, and looked calmly at the pictures on his desk: his wife and his other daughters. Then she looked up, asking, "Am I compromising you by coming here?" "You know Leila, such an attractive single woman . . . , " but while he made light of it, his eyelids twitched and his face was full of anxiety and fear.

"Nothing new, is there, dear? . . . Everything's alright? . . . You have no idea what a relief it is to think that with all the problems I have, at least you are happy. At the end of the year I'll get you something . . . "

Leila said, "I'll get a present for you too." And she thought, "Really, why didn't I bring him something?" She put her hand out to say goodbye, and he kissed it. It was the first time, and while he was bending over, Leila noticed how worn-out and tired he was, how unhappy he looked.

Walking along the street she thought she'd write to Adriano as soon as she got home. But something inside her whispered urgently, "Why not now? . . . Why not right away? . . . It would be more honest—and quicker." So she went into a café, asked for some paper and ink, and wrote, "Dear Adriano, I tried to be forceful, like you told me, but I wasn't able to. I finally understood that whatever my parents might have done to me, I can't blame them now, and instead I only feel deeply sorry for them. And then, all that glitters isn't gold. Their businesses aren't doing well, and maybe, one day, I'll have to take care of them. Instead of making me feel worried or afraid, the thought of this makes me infinitely happy. What more can I say? These feelings just can't be explained. It's clear that our points of view are too different for us to continue to stay together. I'm sorry that you've wasted three years for me, but you're a person with so many fine qualities that you'll easily find someone who's better for you. I'd like to thank you, and send my best regards and friendship.—Leila."

She read over the few lines she'd written several times; they must have given her an unusual sense of satisfaction, because her face became brighter and more radiant, so much so, that after she'd mailed the letter and was on her way to the train station, the men who passed her turned to look at her admiringly. On the train she took off her hat, and could hardly hold back an uncontrollable desire to sing. Standing up straight at the window, mad with joy, she looked at the countryside, which now seemed sweet, soft, extremely beautiful. But why did she feel so bursting with joy? . . . All of a sudden she remembered one of her girlfriends at boarding school who was very smart, always thinking things over. She once asked Leila, "Do you believe it's easy to know whether you love a person or not? . . . It's frightening to think that your marriage and your whole life can be ruined by that small misunderstanding, if a woman thinks she loves someone, when really, she doesn't love him at all." So! . . . She'd thought she loved Adriano, but really she didn't. She detested his flat forehead and cold eyes, his thin, blonde mustache above that small, haughty mouth, his conceitfulness and arrogant wisdom, his voice, his advice. For three years Adriano had kept her in the mean shadow of his egotism, his conniving, his petty resentment; with him she'd wandered in a frightening labyrinth, unable to understand even herself. But now she'd found her way out of it, she was free of him, and free of his cold, oppressive love!

The people in town who saw her get off the train thought, "Miss Leila must be getting married in a week! . . . " And "the mayor's daughters," their mouths fell open when Leila threw her arms around them. "Dear Miss Dele! Dear Miss Genia! But do you realize how beautiful your house is? . . . And your garden!" There's the little garden, all bright and fresh before her, like her whole life—beautiful, splendid, wonderful life!

La stampa
8 December 1929

Fog

Maria Luisa Astaldi

*F*or as long as my cousins were in elementary school she always came to the Pavesa estate to tutor them. My cousins weren't model students, and they always had an exam to take over in October. We would see her off in the distance as she climbed up the hill on the estate, walking under her white umbrella—one of those big, cotton umbrellas that priests and country doctors use.

Her name was Miss Lucia. She had light-colored eyes and a long, pointed face covered with freckles, as if she'd dipped it into a sack of bran.

"You ought to think about getting married. It's high time, Miss Lucia."

Flowers were a passion with her. She grew them herself in a small garden in front of her house that was so bursting with flowers it looked like a tiny cemetery: There were twining jasmine, drooping hydrangea, whimsical little carnations. At one time there were hearty, bright red dahlias too, but she had to give them up because their big, flowery, red heads stuck out of the hedge, and thoughtless boys broke them off to put in their mouths, or behind their ears. The yellow-flowered reseda plants and the morning glories against the wall of the house had grown so lush they blanketed the bedroom window, imprisoning the slats of the shutters. But what did it matter? Miss Lucia didn't really have the nerve to pinch off the little flowering branches and vines. Instead, she lived in the shadowy light, and had given up looking at herself in the mirror.

In summer, the sun is full and blazing as it goes down on the low Lombard plains, and the poplars cast their fragile shadows along the steaming canals in the evening.

The horizon is completely flat, and stretches out with roads that all look alike as each one blurs with the next, with cobblestoned villages, with squat, dilapidated castles gnawed by ivy; but in the evening, great orchestras of frogs and the frantic strains of crickets fill the air. A full, good-natured moon rises in the sky and stops over to one side to listen to the concert, then, happy with the performance, she tosses some small, silver coins into the air; they land in the still water of the canals and shimmer faintly.

The night is full of activity, without mystery or snares. The farmsteads sleep with one eye open: In the middle of the night there's the drum of the milkers, and at four o'clock, before dawn, clanging bells call the stablemen to take care of the animals. The work is endless and unrelenting. It is as if this rich, wakeful land doesn't have the time or desire for dreams. But seeing it in the light of dawn instead, in pale colors and all veiled in fog, with its small, white villages, its slender bell towers, its cloaked castles, and the breathtaking sight of its calm, smooth waters—like a landscape drawn on a cloud—it really seems like a haven for spirits and fairies.

Miss Lucia has so much to do. In winter there's school, in summer there's the garden, and so the years go by. She's not old, and she's not young. It's hard to tell just how old she is.

"She's a sweet girl," my aunt says, "but she seems absent-minded, kind of a scatterbrain. Maybe it's because she's shy."

One time, on Saint Martin's Day*, when my aunt had finished cleaning out the closets and packing the trunks, the little teacher came to tell us goodbye. My aunt introduced her to a salesman who had a suitcase full of fabrics there with him.

"A real bargain." The man was tall and fat, with thick hair and shrewd eyes, and a pencil stuck behind his ear. He opened the suitcase on the table, and a sparkling, frothy skein of veils, silks, and brocatelles in warm spring colors came cascading out.

My aunt tested their softness and strength like an expert.

"These bold shades don't look good on me. They're more suited for you, Miss Lucia. That one would make a beautiful evening dress, or a wedding dress," and she pointed to a flowing piece of white material, trimmed in a haughty taffetalike satin.

---

*A festive day for decanting wine, celebrated on November 11.—TRANS.

The price—according to the salesman—was exceptional, and whoever purchased the full length of fabric would also get another discount. Here you are! He took his pencil from behind his ear and scribbled some figures on the cover of the overturned suitcase, while we kids stood all around the table watching him ecstatically, as if he were a magician.

"What do you say, Miss?"

"I don't go dancing, I don't have the chance. And . . . about my getting married . . . " Her whole face turned deep red, and the bright color melting her freckles made her look younger and more charming. "Who in this village would want to marry me?"

"My dear child, the future is always full of surprises, for all of us. Who can tell? Sooner than you think, in Milan for example, you might meet the young man who's right for you."

"Oh, Madam, I go to Milan so rarely. I stay there only until the next train leaves, just long enough to buy a few things. I don't know anyone there."

"Still, who can tell? Even on a train, at a café, in a store, you could meet the man who'll be your husband. Take my advice, buy this beautiful blue and white dress, and it will bring you good luck."

Maybe my aunt was in a hurry to get rid of the salesman. She was in a good mood and spoke lightheartedly, but I remember that the little school teacher hung on her every word, with a strange excitement that made her nose twitch.

The salesman sang more praises about his goods, worked out more figures, and cut some more prices, and Miss Lucia went skipping away down the hill with her bundle under her arm.

That was the last day we ever saw her.

After that Saint Martin's Day there were long months of frightening and tragic events.

My oldest cousin left for the front, and right away, his first time in action, he was seriously wounded and had to have one of his legs amputated.

It was only after the Armistice, in the spring of 1919, when we were in better spirits and my cousin was able to begin his studies and his life again, that my aunt invited us all to spend Easter at Pavesa.

The estate smelled of mold and abandonment; mice were running around in the attic, and the garden had grown wild and become a meeting place for throngs of cats whose frenzied love calls kept us awake at night.

"And what about Miss Lucia? Hasn't she shown up yet? Let's go find her!"

But we didn't find the little house suffocated by the reseda plants and morning glories, standing inside the small garden that overflowed with flowers like a cemetery. In its place there was some sort of shed, new but already dirty, with plate metal doors and a black sign hanging on the front: "Giordano Bruno* Cooperative."

We asked the warehouseman about her. He was a one-eyed fellow that the town had nicknamed "the doctor" because he was so proud of not speaking in dialect and showed off whenever he could with a pompous eloquence that was riddled with blunders.

"So you haven't heard anything at all about the schoolteacher, Lucia? This winter, poor thing, it happened this winter, just a little after the Cava crossing. She was stone dead, like a squashed frog in the middle of the road. It was the milk truck that ran over her. There was a thick fog, the kind we get around here. You couldn't see past your nose. . . . " Completely satisfied with our grief and attention, he continued his story.

"For a while we couldn't hardly recognize her, Miss Lucia. She'd powder up her face. She'd gotten odd, raving, like they say in other parts. At night people would see her in the garden, pacing up and down like a hen in the henhouse. She'd pick flowers, and put them in her hair and sing, like in church. The boys hid behind the hedge, making fun of her. Then in the evening, around the time for the Ave Maria, she'd go on down the road, in the direction of Cava. She'd sit there on the low wall. When a car came by she'd run into the middle of the road and wave her hands in the air, until the driver had to stop if he didn't want to hit her. Then she'd say, 'Excuse me, Sir, would you give me a ride to Milan?' and she'd hop in. One time it happened to the notary from Mortara, and another time to Anselmo's son, the one from Caseificio. You know how it is, people talked. Then one day, she asked the town gossips with their kids, the postal clerk, me, and the pharmacist all over to her house. She gives everyone candies and sweets, and a glass of sweet wine, just like it was a wedding. 'I'm leaving,' she says. 'I'm getting married. I don't like this village at all anymore. I'm going to live in Milan. I have a fiancé there. Do you want to see my dress?' She goes out, and after a while there she is, coming back in, dressed in white, with some sort of thing on her head like a crown. She looked like the statue of Saint Catherine. The women were all there with their mouths hanging open. 'And now goodbye everyone,' she says. She throws on her shawl, leaves everything the way it is, and off she goes, looking like a ghost in the fog. It was over there, by that row

---

*Giordano Bruno (1548–1600), a writer and philosopher, was arrested in Venice for his revolutionary ideas, tried for heresy by the Inquisition, and burned at the stake.—TRANS.

of trees, after the fork in the road. The men in the truck saw something white moving in the middle of the road, but they couldn't brake in time. The tires ran over her stomach."

"And didn't anybody come to town? Didn't anybody try to find her after she died?"

The one-eyed man shook his head.

"And her fiance?"

"That man hasn't been born yet. It was, like they say, something you'd read in a novel. We found piles of books in her house. She read so much she ruined her brain. Because women aren't like us. Books are bad for them."

Il giornale d'Italia
13 January 1936

The Movies

Ada Negri

She's just a typist, closer to forty than to thirty, not quick and shrewd like so many other working-class women. She slouches a little, and invariably dresses in steel gray or dark brown, with a small felt hat pulled tightly down over her forehead so its shadow will cover her eyes and thin lashes. She's had her hair bobbed like other women, but only so her fine hair—so limp it seems pasted to her head and so thin her braided bun slides out of the hairpins—won't dangle down her neck anymore and embarrass her. Short dresses don't look good on her. They betray her skinny legs, with her nylons obstinately sagging, especially at the ankles. There's nothing that spoils a woman's appearance and makes her more homely than nylons that sag at the ankles.

She lives alone. Her parents are dead, and no young man has ever liked her pale little face, shriveled like an old apple, as if she'd been born with wrinkles. The business office where she works is gloomy, with its electric lights turned on even in the daytime to struggle with the sticky, ashen light coming in the windows overlooking a downtown alley. There's the smell of paper, old and new; numbers; copying ink; of meager, penned-in lives revolving around the daily schedule and payday, the twenty-seventh of the month. The handful of employees have eyes only for the second typist—an adolescent, practically. She has her hair bobbed too, but her lips are lacquered with lipstick, her eyelashes heavy with black mascara, and for a dress she wears a kind of knit beach cover-up that doesn't reach her knees, and clings so tightly to her small breasts and supple hips that it looks as if it were wet.

On Thursday or Saturday evenings, and sometimes on Sunday afternoons, too, the poor little clerk with the wrinkled, applish face goes to the movies.

The other days of the week she thinks about what she saw at the movies, and gets ready for the joy of the next movie.

She goes to the movies without girlfriends, because she doesn't have any. She never looked for friends and didn't find any, not even when she was a little girl going to school. She was always held back by a shyness she couldn't overcome, and also, perhaps, a vague sense of inferiority, an inborn restraint that kept her from opening up about herself, from confiding in someone, from asking for anything. There are some people born with an air that attracts others, and some people born with an air that drives others away. Then there are people with neither one nor the other, and they are the most miserable and lonely of all. Even her name is pitiful: Bigia, which in the Lombard dialect is the corrupted form of the name Luigia, and brings to mind fog, twilight, and rain.

She only wants to go to the best movie theaters where they play the best shows, and that's where she ends up spending half her salary. But isn't it like traveling, after all? Like taking voyages around the world? The only way to travel is first class, with all the comforts. The novelty of it and the feeling of leisure begin at the entrance, in the lobby, which is usually spacious and adorned with columns, lit by heavy, luxurious chandeliers, and decorated with broad stucco moldings, and publicity posters with gigantic headlines and colored drawings done to the nth degree of brightness, a loud, garish style. The film has almost always started already, and, in pitch darkness, the main floor seats seem empty, occupied only by an immense breath of suspense. Sitting in the dark, she often happens to graze the arm of some invisible person; each time the same shiver runs through her. She can't tell whether it's a woman or a man. It's a living being, whose presence she feels, for now, without seeing its face, or being seen herself, and she's not sorry about it. At the intermission, when the lights suddenly come on in the theater, she can see the profile of the man or woman next to her, but she's not interested anymore. To look at someone means to be looked at. She's aware of how shabby and plain she looks. If only it were possible in life to be close to someone all the time without seeing each other!

At the movies she prefers to see dramas in which the most unlikely adventures intertwine and whirl in a vortex around astonishing love affairs. Perhaps this need for flights of fantasy is born from the barrenness and poverty of her own destiny. If she were rich and educated, she'd go to the theater. But being the way she is, the theater—opera or plays—couldn't give her coarse tastes and uncultivated mind the kind of nourishment she relishes at the movies. A fitful, capricious, and often poisoned nourishment. She's not aware of how it happens, but beginning with the first scenes, she completely identifies with the leading lady's character. She enters her world; she loves and hates, sins and takes risks, is joyful, suffers and triumphs, entirely absorbed within the character. For two or three very long and very fleeting, eventful hours, she has Mary Pickford's sweet, affectionate face, Mae Murray's golden halo of hair and wide triangular nostrils, Greta Garbo's lithe body, ambiguous grace, and magical, light blue eyes. She is Pola Negri, she is Bebe Daniels, not as they really are, but as they bring to life the characters they play.

For two or three very long and very fleeting hours she lives in countries she's never seen before but recognizes at first sight and where she feels at ease, as though she'd always lived there. She crosses these lands in luxurious cars and lightning-fast trains, or flies over them in gliders. She stays at hotels worthy of queens and kings, and receives genteel ladies and gentlemen in drawing rooms full of precious objects, she herself adorned and bejeweled, like an idol. Or else, dressed in a low-cut bodice, with a checkered scarf around her neck and a carnation in her hair, she greets adventurers, gold seekers, and jailbirds in a rough American saloon at the edge of the Western prairie. She shakes with fear and fights in worldly intrigues; she risks her life and wins it back; she disappears and reappears. If he's not a Fairbanks-style cowboy or a Ghione-style hoodlum, the man she loves usually behaves nobly and has refined manners, a clean-shaven and perfect face with an enigmatic, scowling smile, and a nervous tic in the left or right corner of his lips. An Anglo-American type, he vaguely resembles the young boss in her office. But her boss is thousands of miles away from her, even when they're separated only by the narrow space between his desk and her typewriter table. Instead, the other man—oh, the other man—is so close to her that she feels the warmth of his breath, and with him she can run away to the farthest ends of the earth.

To run away, to run away to the sea! She's never been there. The only sea she knows is the sea in the movies. She knows it so well that she hears the rhythmic breaking of waves on the beach, she breathes in its saltiness, she relishes its freedom. Only she's bothered by the constant fury of the waves, one rolling in right after the other. Is the sea always so restless, even when it's calm? Everything on the screen happens so fast: the people's gestures, the going, the coming, the crying, the laughing, the rhythm of work, embracing, committing crimes. Everything unfolds in high speed. At the climactic moments of the film, if the theater weren't immersed in darkness, Bigia would see, in the orchestra seats, rows of faces, with their expressions distorted by the rush of blood and the nervous agitation. If she saw herself in a mirror, even her own face would look like this.

If only real life were like life in the movies! With doors that fling open by themselves; paths of water, land, and air, waiting there to rescue whoever is in danger; distances reduced to a dot; nothing forbidden, everything made possible and easy, obeying the crazy whims of fantasy and passion.

But isn't it all lies? And isn't a lie something bad? If Bigia's mother were still alive, it would frighten her. She'd say, "Just look at yourself." But nowadays girls don't listen to their mothers. They say, "I make my own money, so I'll do what I want." But then, Bigia's mother isn't there anymore. No one is there for Bigia, there never will be anyone. A passion burns inside her—although she's never even admitted it to herself and she shows no sign of it; that passion is appeased by the fantastic happenings she enjoys and endures on the screen, and is channeled off in a thousand different directions. She lives two parallel existences; she has two distinct souls. Except that for some time now, the parallel lives have gone astray, they've caught up with each other and intersected. These two souls struggle with one another. When she gets home from the movies, her skin is burning and she has a rapid pulse that comes and goes with a nervous fever. She's not able to fall asleep; she keeps thinking and thinking about images that have the clarity, intensity, and sharpness of hallucinations. Toward dawn, worn out, she finally grows drowsy. But in her sleep, as she dreams, she relives the fable of the weaver who through the magic of love becomes a duchess, or the billionaire who runs away from the splendors of her palace to follow the handsome knight, or the robot woman who's more seductive than a woman of real flesh and blood and drags multitudes to ruin.

It's difficult to wake up again. Her tongue is swollen, her memory tangled, her will weak. In the office she's distracted and sits motionless at the typewriter, daydreaming. She makes mistakes with the figures, amounts to be carried over, and columns. She isn't herself anymore. But maybe she's ill. This is the only thought that keeps the boss from firing her.

One Saturday evening around eleven, she comes out of the Helios movie theater with dazed eyes and a confused buzzing in her ears, her wrinkled applish face transformed by some spellbinding thought that completely absorbs her. In the square, the comings and goings of people pouring out of the nightclubs: they cross each other's paths, horns honk, the haunting glare of signs all lit up in white, purple, deep blue, some in long ribbons, some fanning out, others turning round, like wheels. The car headlights are shining on the wet asphalt. Lights above, lights below. Illusion. She doesn't know where she is. She doesn't know who she is. The climax of the romantic story that elated her just moments ago won't stop playing over and over in front of her eyes and in her mind. Her name is Ginevra. She's twenty years old, in love, desperate. She's waiting on a boulevard in Paris for her lover's car to go by, so she can throw herself in front of it and be crushed. Her lover! He doesn't love her anymore, because he doesn't believe her anymore. Her lover! What sweetness, what pangs, to have a lover, to suffer for love, to cry for him, to say to herself, "Now I'm going to kill myself for him." But not really to die, of course. Instead, she'd be gathered up in his arms, saved by him, and he'd believe in her again, love her again. The heroines in the movies don't actually die, do they?

The scene unfolds as if it were a movie. People pass by and don't look; they're indifferent, in a hurry. Shining lights; vehicles speeding by; everything moving along quickly, without obstacles, as in a dream. Bigia-Ginevra knows she's beautiful, and so elegant, like a porcelain figurine in a Russian gray squirrel fur coat with soft silver flecks, with her legs veiled in a delicate gray mesh, and light pearl gray suede shoes that look like jewels in the mud. She isn't wearing anything on her head. She has a full head of curly blonde hair. Where did she get that blonde head of hair? And how can she see it, if she doesn't have a compact and all the shop windows are shuttered up?

But she's beautiful, elegant, and in love, ready to kill herself.

A fast car swerves sharply but isn't able to avoid the determined victim in time! A scream. Two policemen compassionately lift a woman's body up from the ground. Her shabby little dark brown dress has climbed up to her shoulders in all the havoc, leaving her injured torso and broken legs almost naked. They take her to the hospital in the same car that ran over her. The throng of curious people stares after her. Then they disperse, going their own ways, in different directions.

Someone sighs, "Poor creature!" And another person says, "Who could it be?"

No one. Not really anyone. Just a typist who lived alone and had only one passion—the movies.

Corriere della sera
27 November 1928

A Boy

Pia Rimini

---

*T*he woman caught herself with idle hands as she sat in front of the window, and her dreamy laziness seemed like something to feel guilty about.

To keep her hands busy she unbuttoned and rebuttoned the top of her dress, but even the slightest movement weighed upon her. When she stood up, as if to shake off that sluggishness, she felt the weariness hanging heavily in the air settle in her knees, and she leaned on the windowsill, lost in daydreams.

She rediscovered the feelings of melancholy, the fits of temper, and the weaknesses of adolescence in those deceiving spring days. Chasing after her memories made her feel lazy. As her mind descended backwards through time, she'd lose her thread of thought and pause in the iridescent margin of a fickle indolence, only to be suddenly surprised at feeling like she was her own enemy, and everyone else's enemy too, angry without knowing why, more irritated by not knowing the reason for it than by that vague sense of uneasiness that kept her teetering between tears and outbursts of anger.

She moved away from the window and began to clean up the living room. Her son's mess had a cheerfulness all its own. Books, notebooks, small pens—there wasn't a spot on the table or furniture that wasn't littered with them. The mother stuck her head out the door, "Pietruccio!"

The housekeeper answered from the kitchen, "He's in the courtyard getting some exercise!"

"Tell him to come upstairs!"

She heard the girl answering again, "He says he doesn't want to come in."

"Tell him to come in right away!" As the mother stood still in the breeze coming through the window, she lifted her arms so the wind could play inside her wide sleeves. She ran her fingers through her hair because she liked feeling it ruffle.

Then Pietruccio appeared in the doorway and watched his mother, who blushed and laughed as if she'd been caught doing something wrong. He snapped at her, "Why did you make me come in?"

"You're so flushed!"

The boy moved back brusquely.

"What's wrong?" she said, and straightened his dull blond hair with her fingers.

He shrugged off his mother's hands, so she put them firmly on his shoulders to calm him down, "Is that any way to behave?" She'd taken hold of him and was pushing him toward the small table. "You have history and geography homework to do for tomorrow." As she said this, something about him irritated her. *Such a big, dull, and plain boy. He doesn't take after me at all!* Her voice, which had been soft with affection, became exasperated with anger as the idea leapt to mind: *He's messy and overbearing!*

Distracted, she said, "Who'll go out tonight with Mama if Pietruccio doesn't hurry up and do his homework?"

"Are we going to the movies?" It was as if a burst of sunshine lit up his tanned face. Even his hair seemed to shine, turning blonder, and his gray eyes glinted with gold.

She forgot about how sulky and bad he'd just been. There was something about the boy's enthusiasm and exuberance that reminded her of herself, and she instantly became more tender. She regretted the angry, almost hostile way she'd judged him. *A good looking boy— smart and full of passion!*

Seated at the table, Pietruccio turned around.

"I,"—she heard her voice crack, without knowing why she was on the verge of crying. Every word took her by surprise; every little thing distracted and irritated her. Then, filled with a joy, blushing with shyness she said, "Do your homework," and she sat down. But Pietruccio didn't listen to her.

She lost herself poring over a romance novel that made patches of memories flash, then flicker as she anxiously drew near. Tears quivered on the brims of her eyelashes.

Why doesn't he get here? she thought. *He really did say, 'I'll come see you tomorrow. And we'll talk!'*

She stood up, turning to see if Pietruccio had noticed, and rustled away into the other room. Then she softly closed the door behind her. Later, in the entrance hall, she'd have to be very careful and open the front door just a crack so he wouldn't ring the doorbell when he arrived, and so Pietruccio wouldn't run to see who was there.

The sky had become overcast. She couldn't even see herself in the mirror. To powder her face she had to lean a little closer to the mirror.

How had he put it? . . . ' . . . And we'll talk. . . . '

But what if Pietruccio heard them talking and came into the living room?

Pietruccio's so stubborn! A boy without a father who's grown up like a wild horse! And a mother who's too young, too pretty . . .

Filled with tenderness, she smiled at herself in the mirror through the tears in her eyes.

He said it himself: 'A mother who's too young, too pretty. Pietruccio needs a new father!'

Thunder clouds hung heavily in the air, while the sun's rays slanted through, shedding a harsh light. It was raining. She put her arm outside the window and was more absorbed by the sight of her arm than the weather. A tickle of laughter swelled in her chest.

She slipped down the hall on tiptoes.

"Mama!" she heard Pietruccio call and just at the same time, the doorbell rang.

She ran to the doorway flushed and out of breath, and blurted, "What do you want now?" Her voice had a slight tremor, and a strain of irritation too. As she spoke she tried to listen to the voices and footsteps in the hall. But right away she felt she was betraying herself, and softened her tone of voice, "Hurry up, Pietruccio! Get back to work! I'll be back later."

"Where are you going?"

"Why?" She blushed.

Her eagerness surged with the impatience of a race, the sheer folly of flight imprisoned in still wings. And something of that wild fluttering also spread to her voice.

The boy leapt to his feet. His mother's bewilderment made his bursting rage swell. "Why are you running off?"

But his arrogance made her speak in a strict voice again.

"Why are you making such a scene?" Then all her excitement rushed into scolding him as her anger flared too. "Get to work! Do you understand? If you keep disobeying . . . " and she fell silent, straining to hear.

"But who is it?" said the boy, rushing toward the door to the hall.

The mother blocked his way, "Pietruccio!"

"Let me get by!"

She was his mother, and felt only weakness before him. But she was also a woman, and defended herself. Knowing how far he might go with this, she felt her hands shaking with a vague temptation to slap him.

"I said no. Don't you dare!" She challenged him, shuddering since she knew how blind his fury could be, and thought maybe she could persuade him with kind words. But she also thought that by trying to coax him she'd be giving in to him. Who's in charge: she or he?

The door opened. The housekeeper, drying her hands on her apron, said, "Mr. Ginardi is here. He wants to see you, Ma'am."

The mother saw a flash of anger in the boy's eyes.

"What are you waiting for? Have him come in!" he ordered. Then he lost his patience because the girl didn't give any sign of going.

"Hurry up! You make everybody wait!"

After she'd left the room, the boy asked grimly in a low voice, "What does he want with you?"

"And what does that matter to you?"

The boy tightened his fists: "Why . . . ?" he asked, his voice breaking. Tears were coming to his eyes, and he hid his face with his fists and yelled, crying, "I don't want this! I don't! Tell him to go away! My mama! He wants my mama!"

Instantly disarmed, the mother felt nothing but the boy's pain, the pain of her little boy, and she was drawn to his tears. "But what are you thinking? Pietruccio! Listen! Don't act this way. You don't have any idea. Mr. Ginardi . . . "

At that name, the boy's sobs rose loud and angry.

"He wants to marry me," the mother said quickly. "He's such a good man. And he cares about you, too."

The boy had crouched down on the floor, and at each word the mother said he kicked the small table.

She knelt down beside him and spoke softly, trying to move his hands away from his face, as his tears ran down and dissolved the blotches of ink.

"Now listen! Pay attention!" She walked around nervously. Then, sensing how bitter and hostile he was, she moved over and sat down next to him, a child herself, in all her pain. Now, with her hair messed up, her dress wrinkled, her eyes red from crying, she couldn't go into the living room. And he was waiting for her out there. Between the boy's sobs she heard footsteps pacing up and down in the living room.

Since his mother wasn't saying anything, the boy broke off his crying to glance sideways at her, and he met her eyes. She stood up.

"Don't go!" her son shouted, clutching her skirt. "What does that man want? Why don't you love me?"

Dismayed, the mother leaned on the table. The boy stood up.

"Call Luisa and tell her to send him away!" He coaxed with a meek, ingratiating voice. He sensed that the emotion in those words swayed his mother toward giving in, and he started wheedling her boyishly so he could win her over completely. "Aren't you happy with me? Why do you want him?"

In a tired but kind voice she said, "Go on! Tell Luisa to . . . "

She thought the boy would fly clear to the door. Then she turned around, and the sight of him still crying—looking like such a little boy—made her feel sorry for him. She thought about when he was small and cut his hand. He came running to her, screaming, "Mama!"

"Do you want me to go do it?" she whispered.

The boy didn't answer.

She went over to the door and opened it. Standing in the doorway, she said loudly, "Luisa! Tell Mr. Ginardi . . . ", and her voice broke off. In the silence she heard the boy rushing toward her, his voice nudging at her back softly. She continued, " . . . say I can't, that I don't have time . . . " She quickly stepped back into the room and ran to a corner, where she collapsed into a chair.

The boy heard only her deepening sobs, which she smothered as she hid her face.

"No mama, no . . . " he stammered, feeling a little guilty, but irritated that her tears might ruin his victory. "What do you care about that man? Aren't we happy, just you and me?"

And when he heard the footsteps go down the hall and the sound of the door slamming, he said, "I'll stay with you." And he thought, *Now I'll hurry up and do my homework. Then tonight we'll go to the movies!*

Il giornale d'Italia
19 March 1933

Portrait of a Country Woman

Grazia Deledda

On Saint Michael's Day, in September, the Bilsini family moved to a new home and new land.

They had taken a nine-year lease on a large piece of farmland that was half uncultivated, near the Po River, and they counted on getting a sizable profit out of it with their hard work and determination.

The Bilsini family was a large one, with five children, their widowed mother, and a brother of hers, who called himself the head of the house even though he was half-paralyzed, and didn't have a cent of his own. Actually, he was the one who had advised his sister and nephews to sell their small piece of property so that they could lease the other land. Although once a noble's feudal estate, the land had fallen deeper and deeper into neglect, until it finally became the property of a broom sales-man who had gotten it for almost nothing. So he leased it out at a small price: one hundred and ten lire per *biolca*,* two capons, forty eggs in winter, and a basket of grapes in summer. For years, this land had lain in waste. And yet the Bilsinis were going there as if it were the Promised Land, or better still, as if it were a mine to work for all it was worth, since they knew this was the only place where their youthful vitality and strength could be harnessed and converted into gold.

---

*A system of land measurement used in northern Italy, equivalent to two to three thousand square yards.—TRANS.

One of the widow's sons, the next to the oldest, was doing his military service, and the oldest was already married and had two children. His wife and the youngest of the brothers had left that morning for their new home, taking the first load of family belongings and farm tools. Now the others—with a wagon loaded with furniture, a two-wheeled buggy, the bicycles, the dog, the cat, and the cage with the blackbird inside—were all heading onto a pontoon bridge over the Po River, as they slowly made their way to their destination. The two youngest children, plump, blonde, with cheeks red as ripe apples, were in the wagon between the mattresses and small baskets. Their father, who still looked like a boy himself, with his blonde hair and ruddy face like his children's, watched over them lovingly as they laughed and joked with his other two brothers, who were riding along on their bicycles, one on each side of the wagon.

His uncle and mother followed behind in the buggy. Annalena Bilsini drove the buggy, while keeping a constant eye on everything, to see that it moved along in an orderly fashion. Everything was going fine, when all of a sudden the old, but still spirited, mare pulling the buggy pricked up her ears, signalling that some kind of danger was nearby, and the woman gripped the reins tightly in her large hands, tanned and rough, like a man's.

The procession stopped on the left side of the bridge, while a truck loaded with bags of corn sped by on the right. The whole bridge was shaking, as if it were about to break into pieces, and even the water below rushed by as if whirling with fright. The truck driver, with his face gleaming like bronze in the sunlight, was singing at the top of his lungs, almost as if he were doing a medley with the earthquakelike racket he raised in his wake.

The young Bilsini boys yelled after him, shouting angrily, and the small children in the wagon cried. Their uncle—who had a long beard—sat in the buggy, with his bony hand resting motionless on his knee, as he mumbled, "He's going straight to hell, no doubt about it." Leaning back in her seat, the woman was the only one who watched happily as the truck went on its stormy way; her blue eyes sparkled with joy in her square, ruddy face.

"He's just like my son Pietro," she said, loosening the reins, as if she wanted to take a wild run too. But her brother's mumbling held her back.

"Your son Pietro is a good-looking boy!"

Yes, my Pietro is good looking, she thought, as her face returned to its usual stony expression, hardened by her inflexible will. *He's good looking, but also willful, and unruly. He's the cross I have to bear, the only crooked branch in the family—the only child I couldn't manage to bend to the rules of hard work and sacrifice that our family lives by.*

"Dionisio," she said to her brother, who always seemed to guess her most secret thoughts anyway, "did you know that I got a letter from Pietro? It came just as we were leaving the house. I have it here," she added, touching her bosom. "I'll let you read it later."

"I saw the postman come," old Longbeard said, with a kind of grudging disinterest. "So, what does that character have to say?"

"He says he's fine, he's put on some weight, and he's an orderly for a captain who's a bachelor, who sends him off to walk his horse and take letters and gifts to his fiancée. He goes on to say that he's happy with army life, and is even thinking about signing up again."

"That's great!" the man exclaimed, with satisfaction. But most of all, he was relieved by the news. Then he got to thinking again, and asked, "Does he say anything else?"

"Yes, there's more. As usual, he asks me to send him some money."

"That's great," he repeated, this time in a different tone. Then a heavy silence fell between them.

The mother thought to herself, *Sure, everything is going fine with Pietro. With him you never know whether to hope for him to return or to dread it. His brothers never talk about him. And since you, dear brother, remember how our family went to ruin because of our uncles, who loafed around and gave in to all their weaknesses, like Pietro, you think it's best just to let him alone to lead the life of a lowly soldier. If there's another war, he is sure to make a name for himself and go a long way in the army, because he's not even afraid of being shot. Dear me! I'm the only one who wishes he would come back home. My heart is with you, Pietro, because you're the weakness in my life, the wound that needs to be cared for, dear Pietro, though you're so far away.*

It was easy for her to get lost in tender thoughts about her children because the going was slow. The bridge was gorged with traffic, so everyone had to stop again and again. There were wagons loaded with apples going by that left behind a strong fragrance, as if they were full of beautiful women; there were wagons full of grapes, sorghum, and wicker; there were automobiles with heavy pig merchants reclining inside. The smell of fruit, of newly pressed grapes, of aromatic herbs, and of human bodies—stout, energetic, and active—mingled with the smell of the rich valley bursting with crops, of land actually impregnated with human sweat until it produced with divine abundance.

From their wagon, the Bilsinis, who had barely enough grain for sowing and wheat to get by that year, watched the other wagons loaded with foodstuffs as if they were sacred vehicles and calculated the price of each item without saying a word. The mother and uncle did talk about food and prices as they sat in the family's buggy, which made them think of the eventful trips taken by their ancestors, who were merchants and brokers. When they had to make stops the woman didn't mind; she looked at the scenery and gave in to the wistful call of nostalgia. She had crossed over that bridge, in that same buggy—light, and narrow like a love seat—so many times before, first as a young girl, and then as a bride. Every time she had gone over the bridge, the large river, the shimmering expanse of water and horizon, and the woodlands stretching back from the riverbanks had made her feel a sense of amazement and the desire that one of the pontoons—they were made of wood then—would break away and carry her and the buggy down the river, far away to unknown lands where the river went.

Her desire to go far away, to places she had never been before, surely sprang from the fact that she had never experienced or gotten any pleasure from love.

Because her marriage was one of convenience, to a man who was already old, the only thing she had known of married life was the pain and joy of motherhood. So a sting of desire, the germ of an infectious sadness, flowed in her blood, without her even knowing it. But her love for her children, her ambition to see them rich and happy one day, filled the emptiness in her life.

When all of them finally came to the end of the bridge—the wagon with the children, the cat, the blackbird with round, foolish eyes, the mattresses glowing red in the fire of the sunset—she turned toward the high embankment, which was all green and golden, and then thought about their big, new house, where there was so much work to be done. After looking one last time at the river and the sun, which seemed to dissolve in the glimmering water, she continued the journey, thinking that she had really landed on another shore of her life.

Along the embankment, the ride was more peaceful. The two young Bilsini children, who looked a lot like their mother, with her ruddy skin, her square and willful face, and her deep blue eyes—that shade of blue that was icy but full of goodness and revealed her northern origins— dashed off on their bicycles in a dizzy race along the edge of the embankment and soon disappeared at top speed over the horizon.

Uncle Dionisio repeated his same old, mysterious and fatalistic line, "Off they go . . . off they go . . . "

By that he meant, What's all the hurry for? Off they go, rushing to get somewhere, and they don't understand that it's no use, since we all end up dying sooner or later.

But this time Annalena openly rebelled against him, even getting angry with the mare, who, like everyone else, had been lulled into a slow pace by the monotonous sound of her bell and looked as if she agreed with the old man.

"Let them run ahead, for heaven's sake! If they don't run now, when will they? When they have a cane?"

"You get where you're going just the same."

"That's not so! You get there late when you go slowly. And since we haven't arrived where we're going yet, Dionisio, let's at least give them the chance to get there."

Yet she too yielded once again to the majestic calm of the sunset. It seemed as if the sun itself, as it slowly went down beyond the swirling circle of cultivated fields, was reaching out to her with its rays of light, to hold her strong hand and greet her like a father. Tomorrow we'll see each other again! But when we see each other the next time, it will be different, Annalena Bilsini. Tomorrow you'll be a new woman, on a different path, and I'll be a new sun for you. Farewell.

The clouds of gnats and mosquitoes that had been bothering the travelers disappeared along with the sun. Now everything was quiet; the crimson sky glowed between the poplars beyond the river as if it were a fireplace lit in a beautiful winter's twilight, while the deep green meadows and young groves of trees suspended above the rosy mirror of flowing water recalled springtime.

When the wagon suddenly came down from the embankment, on a sloping road that seemed to sink into the valley, the air, which had abruptly turned gloomy, and the smell of cut millet reminded the woman again of the house, the land, and the work that were waiting for her.

The silence was broken by the sound of the two children bickering in the wagon. The youngest boy was clenching something tightly in his closed fist, and gnashing his small teeth to defend himself better, as he yelled, "It's mine! It's mine! I'm telling you it's mine!"

But since the older boy was fiercely trying to pry open his brother's fingers, and cursing his head off like a little scoundrel, the small boy opened his hand and started to cry, screaming all the while. The large gray dog with long curly fur, began barking noisily, and all of a sudden Annalena stopped the horse.

"Now I'm going to get out of the buggy and tan your bare hides," she yelled in a deep voice. And as the two children had been grabbing and biting each other, she certainly did carry out the threat. She jumped down from the buggy, climbed onto the wheel of the wagon and stretched each one of the quarreling boys out on the mattress; then she pulled down their pants and spanked them so hard their skin turned as red as a drunk's cheeks.

"Now, you ought to get the same treatment, for not teaching your children how to behave," she yelled at the young father, who couldn't believe his eyes.

Uncle Dionisio had kept quiet, but when the woman got up in the buggy again, and started the mare with her cart driver's *giddyup,* he stroked his beard with his healthy hand and announced, "There's going to be trouble between them as long as they're breathing."

"Why should there be? Ever since they were little, my children have always gotten along. That's what I taught them to do, and that's how it has to be. There's strength in unity."

"That's just fine then!" he exclaimed, but he seemed to be making fun of his sister.

When they arrived at their new home, the last glimmer of twilight shone on the front door and on the wall around the threshing floor. This new home, standing alone at the corner of two solitary roads, really was, as they said, a relic of feudal times, old and run-down, with a presumptuous chocolate-colored tower on one side, where the Bilsini daughter-in-law had already settled the pigeons. There were two tall plane-trees in front of the house—one on each side of the front door—and their green leaves, tinged red by the sky's last reflection, cheered up the rather gloomy appearance of the whole place. That same glimmer of light, glowing between the trunks of the plane-trees, revealed a niche in the wall, next to the door, where a little Madonna painted yellow, red, and blue stood holding a doll-like baby Jesus and staring at a small extinguished votive light at her feet.

The first thing that Annalena Bilsini noticed was that small glass that was empty of oil, its wick dead, which showed the kind of condition the house and surrounding land were in before she and her family had arrived. So the first thing she did when she went into the large, messy kitchen was fill the glass with oil. Then she lit the wick, and carried the light to the niche, where she stood and made the sign of the cross.

"I am here now," she told the small Madonna, winking her left eye, as if speaking with an old acquaintance, "so protect my soul, and make my family prosper."

Then she walked from one plane-tree to the other, and touched their trunks, which looked like columns of serpentine marble; in this way, she secured an impenetrable barrier before the door of her home and her new life.

Corriere della sera
25 January 1926

The Pomegranate

Gianna Manzini

*S*ometimes at night, people who've stayed at home don't know what to do, because the evening gets worse moment by moment and presses against the window panes, beckoning for help. It's even hard to speak; just as when a sick person is feeling bad and speaks with words that break off from one another; they are too precise, worse than if they were put down in writing. And they sound just right, with their judgmental tones, coming from the mouths of old people, who gain importance at those times and are listened to.

So Fiore took advantage of the moment to declare, "Children should never be away from home for so many months. Now Sandro doesn't seem like part of the family anymore," and she looked over at the room where the young man was keeping to himself.

Amalia shook her head as if to say, "It wouldn't make a difference anyway." Actually, she believed she hadn't known how to protect him, not even when she'd carried him in her womb. Images, startled jumps, private bursts of joy had disturbed her last slow conversation with the baby who was about to be born. Inescapably then, life, which is impossible for anyone to control, intervened to break the miracle of those two hearts beating harmoniously together so it could secretly mark the little child inside her.

She again saw the wine shop with its small marble tables, and some benches and stools over to one side. Mostly women and old men sat on the benches up against the wall, while she sat between the counter and the shelves of bottles, with her chair turned so that she could keep an eye on the kitchen door and the entrance at the same time.

An old man. He came there every day. He brought along a small bottle of wine in his pocket, but ordered a glass of cheap wine so he'd have an excuse to sit in the shop. He stayed for hours and hours without ever saying a word. As he drank he stared at Amalia. His eyes, as if they'd been hard to peel open, were clouded with blood, like fertilized eggs, yet maliciously lit up as they bore through her more and more intensely, until finally the woman sensed that he'd found something in particular inside her and she was startled, believing the old man had discovered the heart of her unborn son. Not even the shelter of the counter was of any help to her. That stare, bent according to the way he moved his head as he took each gulp of wine, penetrated through her, making a knot—an actual knot—around her child. Perhaps, even in her womb, the baby was becoming less hers, already a little bit stolen.

"It's bad to send them away from home, and even worse to let them study," insisted the grandfather.

"Try to make him talk about it, Amalia," prodded Gemma, an old woman who'd never married, with an urgency that cleared her mind. "You have every right to ask your son questions."

"Is it possible he'd confide in me?" she wondered doubtfully. Then it immediately occurred to her that the day before, at lunch, when the relatives had insisted that Sandro had changed a lot in the two years he'd been away from home (he had defended himself with a steady smile), she'd faintly acquiesced "yes, a little paler," and looked the other way, because to keep on watching someone closely is like presuming you understand. Instead she ought to ask him to forgive her for knowing too much and for knowing in that remote, absolute way that mothers do.

"Is it possible he'd confide in me?" she wondered again. It seemed like her son should reproach her, with good reason, for that kind of second sight, that intuitive way of knowing, like having touched without the danger of thoughts.

All of a sudden she thought she understood Sandro's sense of kindness as she remembered a time when she was pregnant, working in the shop.

One time when she was leaning against the doorjam to rest, the sound of a horse pawing the ground startled her. As she turned around, she saw him collapse gently on his front legs, finally lowering his muzzle between them. Such a peaceful way of falling! Humiliated and resigned, he looked like he didn't ever want to get up again, and it seemed as if he turned all white at that moment. She tried to go to the animal because she wanted to pet him, but she couldn't manage to take even one step. She thought the color was draining from her face and realized she was slowly descending into herself, reaching a spacious, restful place anchored between her hips, where her belly was becoming broader, more generous, already like a mother's. They took her home, unconscious. From then on a new bliss lit up her face, and everyone insisted that she'd become more beautiful.

Then she recalled that one evening two workers had started to argue. In the middle of the shop they were talking face to face, almost speechless. People gathered around them, but nobody knew what was going on. The two men didn't even move a muscle, and finally a crushing silence swelled. So the circle of curious people watching shifted aside. A woman suddenly cried out. It was worse than if they'd shed blood. Instead, the man who was most livid with rage only shot an accusing look at the other angry man. Then he turned around to leave. At the door they each went their separate ways.

"Just like that," she murmured, sure she understood the restrained way Sandro fought within himself and how much effort it took for him to bear it in silence.

Around her they kept on talking about Sandro.

"When he was a little boy and you left him alone for a while, he'd look so glum. You'd think maybe he'd hurt himself and didn't want to tell anyone."

"Do you remember when I gave him that puppet theater? He didn't like those puppets. Maybe they scared him."

Amalia couldn't stand the way they were dredging up things that used to make her son upset when he was little. She wanted to say she didn't like it: *It's like prying to do that. Worse than making someone talk in their sleep.* But she affectionately approved when she heard Gemma bring up the blocks. "And that set of building blocks, with all those pieces? Scattered on the table they really looked like a wreck of castles, of churches and buildings. He liked looking at the booklet better. The one that showed what you could make with those painted blocks."

"You're right. He really got carried away looking at the pictures." And Amalia smiled, not so much at the image of her cheerful son as at the memory of a happy day shortly before he was born.

It was the end of March, in the country. "You need to get some exercise," they'd told her. She walked obediently, not paying attention to how tired she felt. Finally she gave in, and went to rest on an embankment, dangling her legs over it. The reeds, the water in the ditch, some slender trees above the young, green wheat blended together in a spectacle that delighted her. Every sight attained greater meaning and refinement, and she discovered new horizons, each one clearer than the last, which she easily reached, purely through the quickened beating of her heart, with her temples and wrists pulsing, almost deliriously tired. What an extraordinary journey through those sharp images following one right after the other! Such possibility for happiness had undoubtedly become greater in her son.

"And to think that during two years at the university he didn't even go to class once. What could he have done all that time?"

The old, unmarried woman was tormented by a need to know; it made her mouth feel as if she'd bitten into a piece of sour fruit.

Meanwhile Amalia yielded to another memory of the time when she was pregnant.

As she sat behind the counter she saw a cart of pomegranates go by. In the ashen season that fruit announced an exotic gaiety, as if stolen from another life. Out in the open and yet completely secret, they offended the gentle grayness of the sirocco.

In a childish outburst she asked for one, feeling ready to burst into tears.

Her husband wrapped the apron around his waist and went out. He came back a moment later, holding the pomegranate out to her. "Here it is. I chose the best one." Amalia took it and put it on a shelf between some bottles.

All of a sudden the pomegranate tumbled down onto the marble-top counter and split open. With a surprise so great that she still wondered at its intensity, the woman saw the red crack. It startled her, almost as if she recognized a sign that she'd been expecting, and right then an unrestrained joy, quivering and glistening, made her mouth water. She closed the piece of fruit between her palms, but the harder she squeezed it together, the deeper she saw into that juicy, sumptuous red fruit when she let go. She was afraid of it and laughed.

So she thought it was right for Sandro not to be able to answer her questions, even if she'd found the strength to ask them.

After all, what more was there to know? By reviving so much of what she'd felt as a mother, she'd stripped herself of pride.

"It seems like you don't realize you're his mother. It's all up to you to make him talk about it."

"Up to me?" And she was about to add, "What does it matter that I'm his mother?" Instead she took her handkerchief and passed it over her trembling lips.

"Go talk to him," insisted Gemma, in an anxious, urgent voice as she pushed her toward Sandro's room, "and start by chatting about this and that."

A few steps from the door Amalia stopped. Her weary meandering back through memories of the time when she was about to become a mother had made her completely sure of one thing: "Life gets hold of our children before they're even born." Who said this? she asked herself. "I did," and she was astonished. Weak tears, like a child's, wet her face.

Looking at the clock, Fiore announced, "It's time to have dinner."

The evening finally seemed settled. A door opened and Sandro appeared. Cheerfully, quickly wiping away her tears, his mother said, "Do you want to eat in your room tonight?" Then, worried that she might have upset him by showing she had guessed what he really wanted, she added, "It's just that you look tired to me, and we usually talk too much at dinner."

Il giornale d'Italia
19 July 1936

A White Cloud

Gianna Manzini

*I*t was winter. Veiled with flickering tenderness, the sun's rays licked up whatever they fell on; the sun was weak, clinging to everyone's clothing, making their flesh too sensitive. People wanted to console it by gazing up soothingly. All of a sudden, in the sky's clean, cold blue, a ribbon of white cloud appeared, as if it were announcing a birth. We stopped. The piazza was like a ring tightening around us. We had to walk pressed closely against each other.

In a voice that sounded far away from everything, even from me, Vittorio said, "A quiet, almost monotonous life. You'd have just gotten out of bed, and would be lingering at the window. . . . " The shutters of a tall, pink house flew open. With its long rooftop balcony the house leaned out and looked below, helped by ivy and geraniums. "Look, you put the combs on the windowsill to dry. But then you suddenly turn away, just because the baby calls you."

My baby girl! I feel her in my blood as it rises inside me. My blood recognizes her, has felt her for years in its fitful pulse, knowing it could be calmed only if its beating were united with hers. For years! Yet I, bewildered, have just now discovered the face I'll give her; a beautiful face with luscious, blonde hair, light and wavy. Her face resembles the portrait of a boy I saw hanging on the wall of a café, so friendly I smiled at him and could have almost talked with his image. But around her eyes, my daughter doesn't resemble anyone. Her eyes belong entirely to her, they're hers alone, absolutely hers. Around her neck she's wearing a small gold necklace: the benediction. She's not holding a toy. With her hands hanging limply against her pretty, long dress, her eyes pull me toward her.

Suddenly I remembered my mother, who used to tell me, "You didn't want me to stand by the window. You'd cling to my skirt, with that look in your eyes, until one day your papa said, 'We've got to make this little girl stop begging this way. It would be better if she'd cry or talk back.' "

My mother and I were united by this memory in an unexpected way; our same longing for more time bound us to the world. Even many years after her death, she continued to claim the future for me, anxious to be right, somehow, through my life. "Do you see I've reached you?" I felt as if I were whispering to her. The front of that house stirred with awakening; I felt the curtains billow like sails. With so many of its windows now open, the house had become extremely light, and its breath quickened with joy, like mine; it weighed anchor on the current of a full happy day, like I did.

A tall, slender young woman passed by. She had a thin face and light-colored braids resting on her dull gray coat. She was just like my little girl would be in sixteen years. "Before long, she'll get engaged," I said. I began to yearn for more time. To gain time and make it mine I only had to imagine I was a drop of blood on this earth. Years, decades. I traced lines through time as easily as I would have parted my little girl's hair. And I also began to long to be healthy, "Now I'll get all better. Sometimes an idea spins me around, holding me like a leaf in a whirlpool. I have to get over this too."

I saw a baby girl in a carriage pushed by a young man. She was calm. She was smiling. No! I'll want to hold her in my arms, her face level with mine, so what she'll see in front of her will be exactly what I see—people, trees, horses, houses, not a baby carriage's silk sky.

Right from the start, she'll face the world straight on.

(The memory of a precious encounter suddenly comes almost leaping to mind. There's a baby boy in swaddling, held up high in the air in a woman's arms. He touches the ground through the fringe of a large, dark shawl that's wrapped around him. With a hood hanging over his head as if he were a poor, ancient king, he sticks out his small gray face, wrinkled like an idol. He's the peddler's little son. The man walks out in front with his case full of lace, ribbon, skeins, and silk ribbons across his back, while his wife follows behind with the child in her arms, moving in long, slow strides. It's a litany, a procession. That woman walks and walks, taking so much trouble so her son can feast his solemn eyes on all the lively road before him.

Image upon image, the world frolics before the child. It flirts with him, wants to compromise him—be it curiosity or desire filtering through—so that this dazzling beginning may announce the dawn of passion. With colors, shapes, movements, fantasies it calls to him, jostles him, strikes at him, begs him to shed a tear. But serious and impassive, he just watches, with his irisless and steady eyes, gathering himself in a memory that spectacle hasn't muddled yet. Frail, he ploughs through the day with demanding steadfastness. In fact, if the wind should die down with the first shadow of evening, the surrendering world will mysteriously ask for his forgiveness.)

Imagining that I was carrying a child as experienced and victorious as he, I climbed a long stairway as if I were wearing a long train.

As I climbed I murmured, "My mother, me, my little girl . . . : a group, a force. My little girl grows up, becomes engaged, and I turn all white. . . ."

My thoughts returned to my mother. I again saw her window over that street, supported at the top and bottom by two piazzas with carriages, cars, and people going back and forth in a monotonous movement, as if through a sieve. I saw her emerging from the shadows in the room, as she moved with her fair-skinned face and dark hair into the frame of full light. She was free, almost fickle, at her shoulders, her neck and head, while her knees were bound. The bleak darkness of the room held her back and sucked her in; it was a breath, it was a face, it was my father's yearning. She teased him with her silent laughter. My shock extinguished that white flash of light on her face, but it also pushed her into the background, where she was obscured by the bursting sheen of lips and hair.

Slavery without escape. The desire to be hugged came whirling over me. I staggered. My shoulders felt weak, defenseless, drawn to the slope of that interminable stairway—fragile, hollow life. The sky spun over my head, and came down around me slow and steady like the flight of a mean bird. Afloat in the piazza, I was more exposed than an object in a mirror.

Lifted up so high, I thought I had to state my position, to make some decision. Instead, in just an instant and without a word, the future became clear, as when a playing card is turned over.

Vittorio said, "I want something to remember this morning by." The usual strolling photographer appeared. As I twisted my gaze for the lens I thought that, as confident and happy as I was, I could control the image it drank up. But five minutes later, in the photograph I saw a frightened face, betrayed by its eyes, and a tired person driven ahead by an anxiety that was masked unexpectedly by a shadow of coquetry.

Il giornale d'Italia
25 February 1939

A White Cloud   81

A Drama in Silence

Maddalena Crispolti

*H*e stood still in the doorway. All his crowded memories came rushing in on him from the open room, which looked abandoned, like a
place that had no use any more. The bed had a silk blanket over it,
and still bore the impression of the dead woman's body. A few withered
and scorched rose petals lay scattered on the floor, while the mingled
smells of burned church candles and of all the flowers that had filled
the room for almost two days lingered, in spite of the air coming in
through the wide open window and filled his mouth with a bitter, dis-
gusting taste. He stood there, reliving in a few moments the whole story
of her deathly illness, and the whole story of her life. He didn't have
the courage to go through the doorway, just as he didn't have the
courage to move back and close the door to that room. Any other time
he'd have done all these little things without giving them a thought,
but now they seemed as if they were of monumental importance.

He couldn't take his eyes off that bed where his mother had died.
His mother! All he'd had in his life was that sweet woman, a little sad
and withdrawn, but so loving and devoted! That pale figure, that
shadow of a woman had made him the man he was today, a man who
wasn't afraid of life. To protect that defenseless creature he'd developed
a moral virility stronger than any physical power; to make her smile
less sad he'd opened his heart to see everything that was beautiful and
good in life.

And now, would all of this survive in him? Wouldn't the disappearance of that weak creature annihilate the strength that had been born and had grown for her sake?

A shutter swung closed with a mournful, empty sound that startled the young man. He mechanically put his hand up to his forehead. His eyes were dry, without a single tear clouding them, but a shooting pain made his heart ache.

"Mother!" he murmured, and as if he'd called her forth, he saw her again lying there on the bed, just as she'd been in her last moments—pale and helpless, without any more strength, no longer smiling. Again, he saw her eyes wander fearfully around the room as if searching for something she could grab onto, he saw her agitated waxen hands on the white blankets moving in a final spasmodic gesture. Then in the mournful silence he again heard the prayers that rose for her, though she didn't seem to hear them, and later an unbroken, piercing sob.

Who was crying like that? It was their doctor, their friend. For all those years he'd been her doctor, given her advice and support while she was all alone. Now he was crying because he had no way to save her, and meanwhile he, her son, wasn't able to cry.

"Mother!" He repeated again, "Dear mother!" For an instant it seemed as if she'd come back to him and was smiling at him. Then his first tears began to dampen his eyes, and soon streamed down, covering his face. His tears made him feel as if he were a child again who needed to be comforted. But who could help him?

He looked around. No one! He didn't have anyone.

But just as this thought took shape, an image resurfaced in his mind, the image of the man who had been crying there in that same room where the woman had lain in her death agony. But immediately a sense of agonizing repulsion stopped him. No, he wouldn't turn to him!

And the faint image of the man crying stuck in his mind. He was old! He'd always thought of him as old, but now he realized he couldn't be much older than his mother. He remembered how he'd always been right there with them, between the woman—deserted by her husband—and her son . . . a friend, adviser, doctor . . .

A long shiver made him shake. What else had that man been in their life? The woman had always smiled at him, and ever since he was a small boy, he too had learned to smile at the man's sincere face and kind eyes. But not anymore. Now he felt a dull anger toward him rising inside himself. The man's heart-breaking sobs were like a barrier that divided them.

The doorbell echoed sharply through that sad house. The young man pulled himself together, shut the bedroom door hard and turned the key. He came back to life, to his own life.

The doctor was waiting at the door. Though pale, his face had regained its usual expression of strength and energy, and his eyes stared into the young man's with tender affection, as always, while he asked, "What do you intend to do, Nando?"

The young man shook his head, "I don't know yet," he answered.

"Will you stay here?"

"I don't know," the young man repeated.

"Nando!" the man said in a voice full of emotion, "your mother asked me to look after you. So remember that I'm here to help you. I'll do whatever I possibly can."

"Thank you," Nando answered tersely.

As he looked at the doctor it seemed as if he were seeing him that day for the first time. His energetic, strong face was still handsome, despite his age, and the man's hand, which was now resting on his own in a gesture of paternal authority, had the lines of a pure masculinity.

That man had always lived close by the deserted woman, with all his attractive good looks and so charming with his intelligent, quick mind. What about her? . . . How had he looked through her eyes?

Now, neither one of them spoke, and in the silence the man felt the boy running away from him heart and soul; he saw his eyes cloud over with something that grief couldn't explain. A deep sigh rose up in his chest, and the lines on his face instantly looked older, as he murmured, "What's wrong, Nando?"

Nando Corsi wearily passed a hand over his forehead.

"Nothing," he answered curtly.

Then suddenly, as if he couldn't hold in the rush of grief overpowering his soul, he added, "Don't you know what my mother meant to me, doctor?"

The doctor's lips trembled faintly, while he nodded in agreement.

"No, you can't know!" the young man continued, growing more and more upset. "She was purity, virtue, love . . . and now . . . "

What was he saying? He stopped, suddenly shaking. Wasn't voicing his shadow of doubt already an offense to the dead woman?

The other man had lowered his face, and for an instant Nando saw the bowed gray head of an old man before him. But a moment later the doctor looked steadily into his eyes again, with the same expression of deep understanding he'd always shown when looking into his mother's eyes.

What was about to happen?

Nando was afraid of the words he might hear, words that would make that heart-ripping shadow of his doubt grow even darker. He felt some other force pushing against him, against his own will, spying on him. But why? The spirit of the dead woman was between them, and each man was using it as a barrier to hide the feelings in his own heart.

"Thank you," the young man finally said, "thank you for all you've done for my mother and me."

The other man made a gesture, interrupting him.

They sat in silence for a few moments, then the doctor stood up.

"It's all clear then," he said. "If you need anything, all you have to do is call me."

Nando didn't answer. He looked at the man as the man looked at him, and it seemed as if each of them was searching the other for the truth, for something he could be certain about.

Silently, they walked across the room. At the end of the living room the light from the large gilded mirror made them stop. With the curtains pulled over the large windows, the whole room was immersed in shades of gray. And in those muted colors, the two male images reflected in the mirror stared back at Nando and the other man with the same pained eyes, of an identical light shade.

It came to him in a flash! Nando Corsi quickly spun around, and turned on all the lights, until the whole room was flooded with light.

The spell was broken. Next to the man in the fullness of his manhood stood the younger one, who was little more than an adolescent, but had seen a shadow of doubt take the shape of reality in those two images reflected in the mirror.

The man's crying seemed to echo again in his ears, as it had echoed in the dying woman's bedroom.

The woman, his mother, was dead, and all the man's grief, all the son's adoration hadn't been able to keep her memory intact.

Now the two men stood face to face, and their searching eyes held each other's gaze again, but this time in mute, anguished expectation.

Who would say something first?

The young man did. His mother's love, which had been the shining beacon in his life, could not be darkened.

He denied everything—what he saw with his own eyes, what he knew deep down inside was the unquestionable truth. He rejected the love that was being offered to him as if to make up for what life had taken from him, he accepted his isolation, and all so that the maternal image would remain just like the one he'd always seen, just like the one he'd always venerated.

His voice trembled when he shook hands with the man who, until yesterday, had been his most trusted friend, and said only, "Goodbye."

The man understood. Tears shone in his tired eyes. Bent and speechless, he left the house for good, like a man who was guilty.

Il giornale d'Italia
26 November 1934

Discordance

Gianna Manzini

At forty, people bear the pull of the earth differently; undoubtedly, we have too much to remember. This is why high heels give the impression that they're disguising something, not just how a person walks, but a whole way of living. They're irritating and pathetic. Trifles like these are all it takes to make me turn mean and ruin a meeting I've anxiously waited for with all my heart.

I can see her coming toward me with that false stride, tottering between courage and defeat, with her makeup done in unnatural shades, and I can't resist the temptation to undo her smile. (For a moment I succeed at rivetting it on her lips, bright and already killed; then I spoil it and turn it sour, crinkling it up. Finally I make it dissolve in a dampish glimmer above her cheeks.) To do this, I only have to look at her meticulously, or better yet, to pass a surprisingly calm gaze over her face, as if I were redoing some figures, some calculation that never comes out right.

But it doesn't go as planned, because my eyes often make discoveries that move me (those lines around her neck, that I'd never noticed until yesterday, display a sense—by now betrayed—of family, a special modesty that comes with her age). What tenderness, what melancholy.

It's worse when Clara seems beautiful, because she looks beautiful in her own way and not how I think she ought to look. It's a betrayal then, a way of escaping me. That's when I take pleasure in mortifying her. I treat her as if I hated her and enjoy hearing myself speak as if

I were using a stage voice—refined, flatter and clearer than a decal.

I start right in telling her a story from my recent past, something she doesn't know about. Hypocritically discreet, I drop suggestive hints about other women, while acting as if I want to flatter her. ("She was just some beautiful girl. Splendid, with dreamlike flesh that made her unreachable, exalted, shrouded in mystery. To make her submit, then to mar her. . . . It was like living a violent curse. A rough game. Instead, you're so gentle. . . . ")

The other day I said to her, "I need to retrace some old itineraries with you. You see, this street has become a double memory for me. Until yesterday it was called Livia and Serena. From tomorrow on it might only be called Clara."

"Let's hope so," she says, with a politeness that offends me; I understand that by rushing ahead of me and swaying a bit at her waist, she calms herself down. She wants to save, at any cost, the mirage of a joy that's already dying.

"What do you mean by 'let's hope so?' " At best it would be like taking three camera shots on the same frame; there's always a slim chance of obtaining priceless effects.

I don't look at her, because I'm sure the expression on her face would punish me, and I think I can make up for it by joking with her: "You're really not one of those women who come and go in a man's life. You're the kind who stays with him."

My talk hit a chord, and the solemn tone has even struck me, like an illicit knife. I would have liked her to start laughing. Instead she looked me over slowly, almost hoping I'd seem more truthful and composed.

I don't tolerate lessons of any kind, so I declare, piqued, "A man like me mustn't make any prophecies or pledges. I was lying a minute ago when I said you'd stay in my life. I don't know, I don't want to know. During my honeymoon—and I really believed that getting married was supposed to resolve a person's love life with happiness—I had the most passionate adventure. I meet a woman on the pier in Venice. Our eyes fall on each other and it's a surprise for us both as we recognize one another in some other time, and in that same instant we steal away ever so slowly from gloomy dissatisfaction. Do you understand? Hope, that way, is no longer elastic stretched thin into a tomorrow that's always just ahead of you. It snaps back, it turns into a miracle.

"My wife and I get on the steamboat, the woman stays on the pier. Illuminated anguish and a happy foreboding isolate me. As soon as we get off the steamboat I find a way to wait for the next one (by taking a series of pictures of my wife I bring myself to put her at a distance, to keep her frozen in the viewfinder). The woman dressed in light blue arrives and laughs at me—unexpected, open, already mine. In Saint Mark's Square, in the same café, sitting a few tables away from each other. Two hours of running our eyes caressingly over each other as I pass my gaze between my wife's shoulder and the brim of her hat. I've never felt the value of the eye as I did then. That same evening, embracing, without any introductions or the hypocrisy of words. I never saw her again, I don't even know her name. But she's the only woman who has always really stayed mine."

It annoys me to have told the truth this way, by accident, and stirred up a faded image in the recesses of my mind, only to let myself be overcome by it.

Irritated, I go back to the beginning of my discussion.

"You can plainly see how difficult it is to foresee anything at all."

"Absolutely! It's only when people are in love that they deceive themselves, thinking they can defy even destiny. What ridiculous arrogance!"

Her voice, not broken by even a thread of emotion, amazes me. She sounds as if she were sending a telegram. I look at her and sense she's my enemy. Holding her head up high, she looks taller than she really is, and I'm afraid she doesn't love me. Right then, I don't want her to love me anymore. Then I could start all over, to win her over again and make her absolutely mine, with no escape, not even for me.

We're at the top of a bridge. I stop, leaning against the parapet. I take advantage of that particular feeling of solitude, almost a hint of dizziness, that always comes over women on bridges.

By talking to her about herself and accusing her, I dominate her, not so much with the words as with the heated tone I've regained in my voice. I reach her at the level of that abstract forehead of hers (which now seems as if it were up high among the rooftop windows, blinded by the last rays of sunlight), where all too often she takes refuge, deserting her own blood. I bend her, I humiliate her until I burst with anger.

And at this moment, perhaps just because of her face—actually clashing with her rouge, but rediscovered and stung by pain—I really love her.

I love that sense of agony in her years, and as soon as she reveals her brittle fragility to me, it brings out my tenderness along with the need to protect. And all this is so nourishing for me that not even the gnawing desire to question it tempts me anymore.

Like everyone else, I have a close friend. I talk to him about this spell that poisons my meetings with Clara, and how I, no less than she, am the victim. I tell him about episode after episode, and worry about clarifying the things (often pitiful) that motivate my outbursts. Certainly, the high heels, the irritating sight of a new hat (but how can a lover not understand that while her man is waiting for her, he anticipates a certain image of her, and only tolerates its betrayal with a stupefying violence that a woman is never capable of?) and, more often, hearing words and sounds in the way she talks, which echo a world that doesn't belong to me and that I'll never know anything about.

My friend looks at me, and says calmly, "It's the usual snag. Everyone's familiar with it. Only usually, people don't hold on to such trifling debris of love. They get rid of it, they toss it out. But you want to polish it up with constant, careful strokes."

Perhaps he's right. But this obsession with touching certain painful or hidden places in my soul comes from a deep need that's also bound to my special sense of honesty, so I can't allow myself to shrug it off.

Actually, I'd like to be a writer, because by writing, maybe I'd pull myself together.

To describe my love affair with Clara, I'd pretend I was a surgeon. Oh, I wouldn't write in the first person; I'd really have to distance myself from me, so I could see myself.

So, the surgeon and the patient.

In my story, I am fully aware of how important the surgical instruments, the bare light, and the cut of the knife are. I understand the fight to gain a victory at the cost of whatever suffering, and the pride of dominating a life that always holds surprises as it takes the shape of this reality called sickness.

As if she were directly under an operating-room light, stripped of all her secrets, she is there, the patient, waiting moment by moment for salvation from the person who martyrs her.

I operate, and feel something like her mother's hate weighing down upon me.

There, I talked about Clara, the patient. Calling her by name is necessary, and is already a gleam of light that clarifies our situation.

Maybe, if I really kept at it and actually, perhaps, put together this story in which a merciless lucidity ought to accompany a crescendo of excitement, I could finally understand why I'm so preposterously unhappy.

Il giornale d'Italia
6 October 1935

Woman with a Little Girl

Ada Negri

A photograph of medium size on the small table in Maria Serena's living room. Unframed still, maybe it's just arrived, set down between an antique silver snuffbox and a piece of Umbrian majolica pottery.

"Who's this?" I ask distractedly, picking up the picture and glancing over it. Then I correct myself, and say, "Who are they?"

"Don't you know Francesca Alamanni? Haven't you ever seen her here at my house? It's her. It looks just like her. So lifelike! She's with her granddaughter, her son's daughter. A lovely little girl. Look how pretty she is! Her name is Lionella, but everyone in the family calls her Pupetta, Streghetta, Bijou.* Her grandmother adores her, but doesn't live with her son's family. She wants to be on her own and free. She travels a lot."

Now Maria Serena slips out of the room, walking fast as usual. Maria Serena has so much to do. But I don't have anything to do, not anything at all. So I stay in the living room in the company of Francesca Alamanni, holding her picture as she gazes up at me, and the longer she gazes at me, the more I feel her come alive.

It's strange, the power of certain pictures. At first sight they capture your eye, and are fixed in your mind forever. It's like that with some people who've never seen each other before, but meet by chance one

---

*Little doll, little witch, jewel.—TRANS.

day and after just a few words and a handshake they suddenly discover it's as if they've been the closest friends for a hundred years, and will stay that way forever.

Francesca Alamanni's eyes are light blue. They aren't wide, but they look like they are because a motionless teardrop is poised on the brim of her lashes, magnifying her pupil and iris. Perhaps she wasn't aware this tear was there when the lens focused upon her, nor that the faint lines of wrinkles at the corners of her temples—each has its own little story to tell—would come out so visibly. Her face is thin and too long, with delicate nostrils and lips. A tired face, but it still doesn't bear the signs of old age, neither its soft flesh and remoteness, nor its leathery hardness. Actually, her face has something indescribably intense and gentle about it, filled with a love of living. Her face brings to mind (and the tiny wrinkles at the corners of her temples aren't important) those large white roses used in vases, the kind that last for ever and ever and don't yellow before losing their petals, but drop them, one by one, unwithered.

Her hair, which must have been blonde but now looks like more of an ashy shade than blonde, is divided into two wavy bands like a halo around her head. I can tell by the delicate way her fur mantle hangs loosely over her shoulders, leaving her neck bare and brightened by a string of pearls, that she's a woman of the upper class who's always lived among things of beauty and sparkle, noble lines, and elegant habits. But under her chin, the pearls don't manage (nor do they try) to hide the dispassionate accusation of age. As she holds the girl's little body at her hips to display it proudly, the skin on her hands stretches over protruding knuckles, and her bones grow thinner, longer, revealing pain and affection mingled inseparably together.

From these hands, the small girl, who's maybe three or four years old, blossoms like a lily.

She's beautiful.

She stands straight and solid, with her velvety head of hair, a mouth like a cherry, round cheeks, large eyes that are calm and clear. Wearing a light sleeveless dress, she shows an air of self-confidence and command that rich, healthy, well-loved children have today. She seems to say: "Everything is mine and I am everything. Here I am."

Yet I sense that the grandmother's hands, suffused with refined vitality, hold her like we hold something that's dear to our heart, but isn't really ours, that hasn't sprung from our own desire and isn't bound up with our need to exist. There's a clear detachment between the woman, who's still beautiful, and the little girl, who promises to become very beautiful. The space of an entire generation wasting away—no one knowing whether its harvest was reaped or lost—stands between them.

If Francesca Alamanni compared how she looks in this photo with an old picture of herself when she was a new mother holding her baby boy in her arms, oh, she'd see how different she was in the old one, even though her face and pose are similar; how much more harmonious and sincere the understanding between mother and son.

Thirty years have gone by. I read in the woman's eyes that she's lived them all in the hope that tomorrow would bring the gift she didn't receive today. Even she didn't know exactly what the gift would be—or yes, she knew but didn't dare admit it to herself. It had to come, it would come. Otherwise, what reason would there have been for living?

It didn't come. I see this too. And it won't come because it's now too late.

Her son has become a man. He worked very hard to win his own place in the world, and moved his mother aside little by little (it goes without saying, the tender wisdom with which children manage to move mothers aside). He got married and had a little girl—this little girl. A living jewel, whose tantrums are more delightful than her charms, whose bossiness and apologies bring showers of kisses down upon her. She's completely her papa and mama's little girl. Papa and mama spoil her, thinking they're bringing her up "in their own way," and heaven help her grandmother if she dares to say anything. All she can do is touch her gently to little purpose, and treat her as if she were a doll that breathes, smiles, and plays. Then the doll will grow up too. One fine morning she'll wake up engaged, and another day she'll be a bride. Really, time goes by faster and faster, the years seem like days, the days seem like hours. And Pupetta-Streghetta-Bijou will go away, following her destiny without looking back. Isn't it like that for everyone?

I press the borders of the photograph lightly between my fingers; I'm enjoying myself and suffering as I decipher it according to my own heart.

Beneath the richness of the sable and the luminosity of the pearls lie the nerves of a dissatisfied woman, painfully shaken and exposed by the excessive refinements of life, both physical and spiritual. All the apparent splendors but no real joy, the kind of joy that makes a child grow like a fruit to perfect maturity, nourished to its fill on its own vital fluid. The eternal misunderstanding between the flesh, which withers, declines and decays, and an inner youthfulness that defies the forward march of time, obeying the obscure law that makes a woman's soul more youthful and passionate as she becomes more experienced—while condemning her body.

That's why she has that motionless tear in her eye that gives her gaze the perplexity of a question without an answer; it's also why the skin on her face and neck looks tired, yet rich with an indescribable radiance below, that stirs like a silent call of love, but love isn't possible anymore. It's why her hands hold the little girl like she's a possession someone else has allowed her to have for just a little while, out of pity. Indeed, it is not that something (but what?) that for years and years made the woman deceive herself into thinking she'd received life as if it were a pawn. That something she has now given up hope of having.

Francesca Alamanni, do you want us to talk a while together? You and me, woman to woman? No one has ever understood anything about us women, and we're too proud to speak out loudly about our secret pain, naked and raw as it is. But if you entrust yourself to my heart, perhaps you will see your own in a mirror. And I'll be able to say the right words to comfort you, if I can't suggest a remedy. There is no remedy, Francesca Alamanni, except to leave it in God's hands.

Corriere della sera
5 December 1926

A Life Story?*

Clarice Tartufari

Last autumn while I was on vacation, I happened to come across a large photo album solidly bound in leather, in the drawing room of a family I was friends with. I was interested in the faces and shapes mounted on the pages, of those people from a time gone by, who were young when their pictures were taken and were now either dead or disowned by life.

The woman of the house was sitting beside me. A beautiful woman in her early fifties, she was like those rose-pink apples preserved for winter under grain that get a little wrinkled, but keep their tastiness.

"This is the album with pictures of people from my father and mother's generation, poor dears. When we divided their things among us children, I got the album. I keep it to remember them by."

"Who's this woman?" I asked, pointing to the picture of a pretty young woman wearing a white veil, with a garland of flowers around her head and a prayer book in her hands.

"My mother, on the day of her First Communion."

"And this blossoming woman, with the deep neckline and open parasol?"

---

*The word *storia* here may mean history or story, and thus captures nuances concerning the nature of and relationship between different kinds of histories, public and personal.—TRANS.

"My mother after her third child. I wasn't born yet."

"She was beautiful, wasn't she?"

"She certainly wasn't unattractive. People who knew her when she was a young woman and also knew me when I was a young girl said we looked a lot alike."

"Is she dead?"

"She died a long time ago, even before my father. She'd be over eighty years old now."

"What was her name?"

The woman hesitated a moment, almost as if she had to think back, then she quickly answered, "Fabiola—an unusual name. If it weren't my mother's, I wouldn't be able to remember it."

After that visit I went to take my usual walk in the country. As I walked alone on a grassy path between two hedges, I amused myself by imagining that woman's story. She'd be over eighty years old now and has been dead a long time, and her name was Fabiola.

So here is the story I told myself, walking alone in the country one gray afternoon last autumn.

In a spacious drawing room of a large house in old papal Rome, a little girl by the name of Fabiola turned seven years old. She sat in a small chair, in front of a bigger chair where a sewing case lay open like a book. It was a present from her father, an antiques dealer in a store near the Spanish Steps.

The little girl was playing with all the pretty gold-plated silver objects, taking them out of the compartments of the case, which was lined with sky blue satin, and putting them back again.

At the same time she listened as her mother, who was sitting on a settee with animal shaped legs, talked with a woman who was a friend of hers. First they talked about Pope Pius IX, who had been forced to escape, and about Garibaldi and the red shirts, and how the foreigners were afraid and didn't come there anymore, making business bad.*

Then they started to talk about her, Fabiola.

"So she's already seven years old now," her mother was saying. "It

---

*Pope Pius IX (1792–1878) fled Rome in the midst of popular uprisings; in 1849 Rome was proclaimed the Roman Republic. Giuseppe Garibaldi (1807–1882) defended the Roman Republic in 1849 with his followers, the red shirts, and in 1860 led the expedition of some one thousand volunteers to Sicily, liberating the island and southern Italian peninsula from foreign rule, and facilitating the political unification of Italy, with Victor Emmanuel II as its king. —TRANS.

seems like yesterday that I was seven years old too! Time flies by. It has wings!"

"You're right, time flies by," her friend repeated sadly.

"It always flies by and you can't ever get it back again!"

"And it takes so many things away with it!" added her mother, shaking her head.

"It takes everything away," the woman said and lifted the hem of her black dress. "What did it ever leave me?"

Fabiola listened drowsily, as if she were dreaming, but tried hard to keep herself awake so she could look more closely at the tiny pair of scissors—they seemed alive, with their two blades like a sharp beak, and the two circles like deep eye sockets where the sky blue satin gazed out so brightly that it made a strong impression on Fabiola.

After that evening a strange confusion between clocks and cages was caught in her imagination, and she'd often stop, deep in thought, to look at the clock in the bedroom. It never moved under the bell jar, even though its hands inched along day and night, and it ticked away constantly.

She imagined there really must have been a little bird inside, moving its wings all the time. Fabiola was sure about this, but it didn't make sense anymore when she was away at school with the nuns. The clock was no longer a merry little bird flapping its wings. Instead, it was a stuffed bird that, like all embalmed animals, looked like it was alive but could not move.

She asked her mother to explain it. "Why is it that sometimes time has wings, and sometimes it doesn't?"

For reasons of her own, her mother's heart was overflowing with bitterness, and she answered in a mocking voice, "Ah! You're saying that there are times when time flies by and others when it doesn't? You'll find out! You'll find out! Just so you know, time doesn't forget about us, not even when we forget about it."

In fact, on a summer night Fabiola realized with immense joy that time hadn't forgotten about her, when she quite unexpectedly understood that she'd become a new person.

That night, at a gathering of friends and relatives, the young people in the party had passionately discussed great events up in Lombardy—the king of Piedmont; the French emperor; Austria, which was forced to evacuate.*

Maybe this news had something to do with it, or maybe it had noth-

---

*In 1859 Italy fought the Second War of Independence, weakening the dominating rule of Austria, which withdrew garrisons from Romagna, but occupied Venetia until 1866, when the region was annexed to Italy.—TRANS.

ing at all to do with it, but that night Fabiola couldn't lie quietly in bed while everyone else in the house was sleeping. Even though she felt happy, she sighed heavily time and again. Filled with amazement, she flung open the window and hid her face in her hands; she smiled to herself, dismayed and proud at the thought that the stars could see the rosy nudity of her arms.

From that exquisite hour on, the world became a garden for Fabiola. She saw flowers everywhere she turned, and when wise people around her said that life is woven from deceptions, Fabiola would laugh, because life was as beautiful and alluring as she was young and carefree, and it walked by her side with a triumphant step.

Hopes dressed in cheerful colors beckoned her, frolicking before her, and it seemed as if all the young men who approached her were slaves before a queen.

Of all the flowers, she liked roses the best, and they brought her good luck. When she had to go to a party for a baptism, she wanted a rose-colored ribbon to put around the waist of her white lace dress, so she went with a widowed aunt of hers to buy it in the most famous fashion house, in Piazza Pasquino.

Attracted by how charming Fabiola was, the owner himself wanted the honor of helping her personally, and he unrolled the wide ribbon from the cardboard roll. The tatting ribbon lay gathered together quivering on the counter, and the young owner lifted it up so they could admire its shade; he squeezed it tightly in his hand so they could see how soft and easy it was to work with. Meanwhile, Fabiola blushed uncontrollably, and couldn't avoid the look in his persuasive eyes.

From then on the widowed aunt, a shrewd woman who was pleased to help, was kept busy accompanying her niece on shopping trips. On these occasions Fabiola pushed ahead with determination, her small feet in high ankle boots with a velvet toe and a silk tassel in the middle of the lacing. Her quick, small feet carried her almost instinctively to the street where the store was. The owner would rush over to the counter, and from the shelves he'd carefully take down frothy laces, which rippled faintly while quivering sighs rose from each side of the counter.

Finally, a mysterious letter, sealed with blue hearts at each of its four corners, arrived for Fabiola.

Fabiola had never read any kind of poetry, but Dante's tercets or Ariosto's octaves wouldn't have been able to evoke a more intense, loftier reverie of feelings and thoughts than that produced by each syllable, relished one by one, of the words in that first love letter.

Another letter, addressed to the proper person, arrived at the same time, containing a succinct, clear statement of the suitor's honest intentions and economic situation.

Prose and poetry being in perfect harmony, the marriage was arranged, the engagement announced.

In that period of her life, time seemed unreal for Fabiola. It was really as if the little bird Belverde had come from the kingdom of fairy tales. Since her fiancé harbored a secret love for Italy, Fabiola felt she loved this great clear word too. So one day when she asked her fiancé why he was sad, and he answered that Garibaldi's followers had been beaten at Mentana, she felt a confused pain. But after the wedding and the magnificent reception, when she was alone with her husband in a carriage pulled by two galloping horses toward Frascati, she forgot the world and herself as his two powerful arms held her tightly and his insistent lips sent an inebriating sweet wine running through her veins. Sun, trees, waterfalls, the sky's wide horizon, the rolling hills were for her nothing but a vision of tumultuous happiness and the voice of her stormy blood. She felt long shivers and unexpected pauses, and looked for shelter against her husband's chest, as he whispered sweet words in her ear and stroked her hair.

She awoke from her dream feeling sick all over, her throat tight with an unbearable repulsion for foods, which all seemed sour to her, and for smells, which all seemed nauseating.

A son was born and others followed. Time flew over the world as if on the wing of a storm; the French Empire was crumbling, the German Empire was rising. But Fabiola, caught up as she was in the little things happening around her, didn't weigh the grandeur of those events. Her oldest child was trying his best to walk. He would tumble down, hit his forehead, and scream dreadfully. Her youngest child refused to nurse, and she inconsolably and with no success squeezed milk from her nipple onto his tightly closed little mouth. Then, while King Victor Emmanuel sent his bersaglieri into Rome,* and the Tiber, overflowing its embankments and rising over bridges, took possession of the city's piazzas and streets, the scarlet hand of German measles touched the swarm of children and Fabiola thought about just one thing: that her small children not get a chill.

Another five children were born, all of them rushing to grow up quickly. The scissors had to keep busily traveling up and down pieces of material; the needle found no rest from its tiny antlike bites; the iron had to push its hot, shiny point wisely over the creases of little winter jackets or ruffles of little fluttering skirts.

When one by one each of her children turned seven, she'd say to her husband, "So the child is already seven years old. It seems like

---

*King Victor Emmanuel II and his army entered Rome in 1870; following a plebescite, Rome, previously part of the Papal states, was united with Italy and soon made its capital.

yesterday that I was seven years old too." And the image of her dead mother, surrounded by shadows, slipped across the back of her memory.

For a confirmation, she wanted to use that famous rose-colored ribbon she'd bought at a time in her life she couldn't forget. The ribbon, carefully folded, was wrapped in a sheet of tissue paper, and the paper was wrapped in a fine cambric handkerchief, which lay delicately on a layer of cotton inside a tightly closed box. Even so, when Fabiola unwrapped the ribbon, she discovered it was faded and frayed. As she sadly folded it up again, she thought to herself that no matter how well someone might take care of something and hide it away, time finds it, touches it, and leaves its signs.

Little by little, one at a time, her sons went away on life's paths and her daughters got married. So Fabiola was alone again with her husband, like at the start of her marriage, but now it was different. Yet tenderness survived.

Her husband, retired from business, was finally dedicating himself to politics, an unfulfilled passion in his life. He read history books, which are, after all, the results of our fathers' politics, and the news about unending congresses, electoral battles, strikes, and so on, which are the history we live. Since she saw the newspapers lying open on the tables and saw her husband taking such a keen interest in them, Fabiola finally became interested in them too, and discussed them no less well than any other woman.

When the disgrace of Adua* fell heavily upon Italy, she fervently said to her husband, who just couldn't accept it, "We have to be strong. God won't allow our children to spend their whole lives under the weight of such humiliation."

As she got out of bed one morning, she realized she'd forgotten about time, but it had never forgotten about her. Now it flew around her, flying so close and so slow she could count the times it went round. She felt an infinite weariness, and only the earth's bosom could give her weary body the rest she needed.

Time flew for an instant around her name, then it went beyond, taking away the memory of Fabiola even from the heart of her youngest daughter, a daughter she'd loved with all-consuming love and who now had to search her memory to remember that her mother's name was Fabiola.

Il giornale d'Italia
15 February 1925

---

*The Battle of Adua (1896) took place in Ethiopia, and was an attempt to expand Italian colonies that saw the Ethiopians defeat the Italians.—TRANS.

Afterword

As she got out of bed one morning, she realized she'd forgotten about time, but it had never forgotten about her. Now it flew around her, flying so close and so slow she could count the times it went round. She felt an infinite weariness, and only the earth's bosom could give her weary body the rest she needed.

Time flew for an instant around her name, then it went beyond, taking away the memory of Fabiola even from the heart of her youngest daughter, a daughter she'd loved with all-consuming love and who now had to search her memory to remember that her mother's name was Fabiola.

—Clarice Tartufari, "A Life Story?", 1925

*L*ike the heroine of her story, Clarice Tartufari (1868–1933) was an aging woman herself when, at fifty-seven, she wrote "A Life Story?" a few years before her death in 1933. In an uncanny way Tartufari's story foretells the fate of its author and of many women writers whose names have been erased from histories of Italian culture during Fascism. By the time Tartufari wrote "A Life Story?" her name regularly appeared in critical essays and newspaper reviews praising her accomplished work as playwright, short story writer, and novelist, which would, according to critics of her time, guarantee her place in Italian literary history. Yet, if we look to histories of Italian literature, anthologies, and critical essays written during the postwar period, with few exceptions we will not find any mention of Clarice Tartufari.[1]

Like Tartufari, such authors as Maria Luisa Astaldi (1900–?), Grazia Deledda (1871–1936), Amalia Guglielminetti (1881–1941), Gianna Manzini (1896–1974), Ada Negri (1870–1945), and Carola Prosperi (1883–?) made a prominent space for themselves in Italian culture prior to and during the Fascist years. Their poetry, novels, and short fiction, which were published in volume form, literary journals, women's publications, and the daily press, generated notable attention among the critical establishment and growing mass readership. The wide circulation of their writing allowed these women to speak to different sectors of an audience whose economic means, as well as tastes, shaped their reading choices. In the varied media utilized by women in the twenties and thirties, more women's texts were being published and read than ever before. Readers of women's writing could identify with authors whose life's work valorized female intellectual and creative powers and with representations of modern female identity, experience, and desire generally repressed by the model of the "New Woman" as exemplary wife and mother, which Mussolini publicized as the exclusive way for women to fulfill their social and political mission in the Fascist regime.

Despite the significant contribution women writers made to Italian life and culture during the dictatorship, their voices have been silenced. Surprisingly, the subject of women's writing produced in the twenties and thirties was repressed not by policies designed to manage culture during Fascism, but by the postwar critical establishment, which either omitted female writers or dismissed them in accounts of culture and literature in the Fascist State, alleging that women merely "reproduced" conservative ideology. Thus, scholars are faced with the irony that postwar literary criticism managed to accomplish the work of Fascist ideologues: to marginalize women writers who generated sustained attention among prominent critics and the general reading public. In this essay I provide an initial reconstruction of this period of women's writing, which is conventionally represented as a gap in the history of Italian women's literature. I suggest that a rereading of the texts both established and new women authors wrote during Fascism—as well as the commentary they generated—calls for a revision of traditional views of these writers' significance in Italian literature, politics, and society. I also examine some crucial issues women's literature of the interwar years raises about periodization, the canon, modernism, neorealism, and postwar theories of literature.

Periodization and canon formation have greatly contributed to the collective disappearance of women writers from histories of the Fascist period. To be sure, Grazia Deledda, recipient of the Nobel Prize for Literature in 1926, generally appears in histories of modern Italian literature. But her classification as a fin-de-siècle writer elides the challenges her later novels and short fiction posed to masculine culture during Fascism. (That anthologies on the interwar period include Luigi Pirandello—who was born in 1867, received the Nobel Prize for Literature in 1934, and died the same year as Deledda—is indicative of how the literary establishment has tended to privilege the metaphysical problems of manhood over the material and psychological conditions of women.) Inclusion in literary history is by no means guaranteed in the cases of Astaldi, Guglielminetti, Negri, and Prosperi, although the content and expressive forms of their literature warranted the close analysis of Benedetto Croce, Giuseppe Antonio Borgese, and Pietro Pancrazi, among other critics esteemed in the twenties and thirties. Of Maddalena Crispolti, Marinella Lodi, and Pia Rimini we know only what their stories say to us.[2] Yet, there is no doubt that these writers captured the attention of a popular audience, since this was a prerequisite for contributing fiction to the cultural page of Italian newspapers. Ironically, if recent scholarship and anthologies are any indication, we know more about Italian women writers of the Renaissance than we do about critically acclaimed and popular women writing in the years of Fascism.[3]

The politics of literary assessment specific to Italian culture following World War II profoundly repressed the subject of women's literature produced during Fascism, and continues to determine which works we read and how we think about writing of this period. Along with the general tendency among young intellectuals of the Left to disavow the merit of literature written in the repressive regime, critics deployed the notion of "pure" or "autonomous" art—the dominant aesthetic of the twenties and thirties—both to define the literary imperatives of their predecessors and to highlight the newness of the counter-aesthetic they proposed, "committed art." Contending that major authors and poets of the Fascist period conceived of literature as transcending personal, social, and political conditions, younger writers, who had grown up during Fascism, and in many cases fought in the Resistance movement, argued for sociopolitical commitment as a literary ideal. Many authors identified with this change of consciousness, which was attributed to the experience of the war, as described by Giaime Pintor (1919–1943):

> If not for the war, I would have continued to be an intellectual with primarily literary interests, I would have looked only for subjects that deeply interested me in the history of man, and a meeting with a young woman or any imaginative impulse would have meant more to me than any political party or doctrine. . . . There comes a time when intellectuals must be able to apply their experience to the sphere of common good, and each must know how to take his place in a combat unit. (*Il sangue d'Europa* [The blood of Europe], 159)[4]

Elaborating on the themes Pintor introduced, avant-garde intellectuals of the forties called for nothing less than a radically "new" conception of the writer as totally committed to society. Literary writing was intended to mediate the changing economic, social, and political conditions of a post–Fascist Italy for the popular classes, and thus rejuvenate Italian culture. Avant-garde writers of the neorealist generation, whose formative works date back to the 1930s, significantly influenced canon formation by formally theorizing writers' new ways of addressing popular readers. However, for all its professed newness, this theory of literature is predicated on a critically constructed rupture with its past. Thus, from a vantage point anchored in the experiences of the war and Resistance, authors and critics looking back on the literature of the Fascist period emphasized those features—detachment from the lower classes, lack of interest in social problems, the use of rhetorical and obtuse language—that contrasted with their own theory of writing as a sociopolitical practice.

In the process, the construction of literary periods excluded women's literature of the twenties and thirties. Since women crafted personal, frank narrative forms to speak to general readers about their own experiences of Italian life and society, the dichotomy between "pure" and "committed" art facilitated, if not required, the omission of female authors from discussions of the Fascist period.[5] Thus, the same male names and texts predictably appear in anthologies and historical commentary on life, culture, and literature during the Fascist regime. It matters little whether these histories address an Italian or English audience. For instance, in his frequently cited study *The Fascist Experience* (1972), Edward R. Tannenbaum maintains that writers who had achieved critical stature prior to Fascism "became increasingly detached from civic and social life and concerned themselves primarily with aesthetic and 'metaphysical' problems" (252). His examples necessarily include Massimo Bontempelli, Emilio Cecchi, Luigi Pirandello, and such poets as Giuseppe Ungaretti and Eugenio Montale. Tannenbaum concludes his observations on literature of the Fascist period with the image of an elite group of male intellectuals writing for themselves, who "became more aloof than ever from the masses and moved in an increasingly limited world of little reviews, hermetic poetry, and isolated artistic experimentation" (274). From this perspective, the "neorealist" conception of the writer's role—involving "a renovation of taste, and a change from a commitment to words to a commitment to things, to man and his society" (270)—would appear radically different.[6]

While the paradigm opposing "pure art" and socially "committed art" has unquestionably forestalled a fuller understanding of the ideological significance of men's literature under Fascism, it has doubly marginalized women's literature of the period, which has been misrepresented in some cases, but most often excluded. Given the multitude of critical studies available in English and Italian, contemporary readers may easily challenge traditional approaches to such writers as Cecchi, Montale, and Pirandello. Obviously, the situation is very different for Negri, Guglielminetti, and Tartufari, among other women writers, since their work has not been widely studied by literary scholars in Italy—let alone those abroad. Although Manacorda does devote attention to Grazia Deledda and Gianna Manzini in his important 1980 study *Storia della letteratura italiana tra le due guerre 1919–1943* (History of Italian literature between the two wars 1919-1943), he represents Deledda as a "writer by instinct" and describes Manzini's literary development as "autonomous." By appropriating their voices and by separating them from the broader sociohistorical and literary context of women's writing, these characterizations obscure how Deledda and Manzini challenge the canon.

What would happen if we tested the critical representations of literature written during Fascism against the stories women told? Was literature, as Lino Pertile claims, primarily "the expression of high culture and the exclusive concern of an elite that considered itself superior to, and remote from, ordinary people" ("Fascism and Literature," 162)? Was the language of fiction and poetry pompous, bookish, rhetorical, and obscure? And what of readers addressed? Would it be accurate to argue, as J. R. Woodhouse does, that in the postwar years "for the first time in the history of Italian literature, a concerted attempt was being made by groups of the country's most gifted and cultured individuals to write and work for a popular audience" (in J. H. Whitfield's *A Short History of Italian Literature*, 319)?

Together with the literary criticism of the time, the short stories in this collection—which represent a sampling of the rich spectrum of ideas, motifs, and narrative modes women writers employed—clearly inscribe the presence of a different aesthetic. Women's literature produced during Fascism exhibits a marked predilection for subjects originating in women's personal, social, and political experience of daily living in patriarchal society. Moreover, in order both to convey their most intimate thoughts and emotions and to speak to a broad readership, these writers crafted new expressive forms that incorporated to varying degrees vocabulary, expressions, and rhetorical patterns of the spoken language.[7] I do not wish to argue, however, that the aesthetic elaborated by women writing during the dictatorship originated with Fascism or was somehow peculiar to the twenty years of Mussolini's rule. On the contrary, I propose that the ways these women write about female experiences of childhood, adolescence, marital union, motherhood, aging, sexuality, and self-determination have precedents in writing of the turn of the century. During Fascism, however, women's critical rewritings of ideal womanhood answered female readers' needs for nontraditional social and cultural models of female self-expression, otherwise censured in writing of their time.

Thus far, commentary on women's literature written during Fascism has tended to rely on historical studies of the seventies, which ambitiously endeavored to examine Fascist efforts to oppress women and align them with the regime's sexual politics.[8] While such research tells much about the construction of woman in Fascist ideology, policy, and propaganda, it tells little about how modern women themselves thought or spoke, or how they may have then negotiated or transgressed patriarchal codes. As a consequence, such studies portray women as objects of repression, forced into resigned silence, or as objects of ideological seduction, coerced into reproducing the patriarchal notion of woman. Yet, more recent historical studies including *How Fascism Ruled Women* by Victoria de Grazia, *Fascism in Popular Memory* by Luisa Passerini, *Rethinking Italian Fascism*, edited by David Forgacs, and *La corporazione delle donne* (The association of women), edited by Marina Addis Saba, have enabled analysis of women's diverse gender roles and their complex relations to what they read and what was said about them. Shifting the terms of debate from "consent" and "resistance," these current studies focus on how the practices of daily living contradict Fascist ideology. Similarly, by examining women's writing and reading we see a different discourse on female identity, sexuality, traditional gender roles, and societal institutions, which transgresses conservative models of femininity. The conceptualization of women as writing, thinking subjects during Fascism provides a long overdue critical framework for understanding how the modes of self-representation, address to readers, and narrative forms women writers elaborated in this period diverged from the work of male writers and Fascist ideologues.

Ample evidence exists to support the idea that women writers comprised a significant presence that challenged male cultural authority during Fascism. The community of women writing in Italy—including established figures like Deledda, Guglielminetti, and Negri as well as new popular authors—increased in the twenties and thirties, building on achievements initiated in the late nineteenth century. Certainly there were more opportunities for women to pursue writing careers after World War I, due in part to the increased markets for fiction created by magazines, local and nationally distributed dailies, and the flourishing women's press, all of which sought to capture their share of an emergent mass readership generally unable to afford books.[9] The sustained commitment to literary enterprises among a growing variety of female authors contradicts the notion that women were disuaded, through ideological persuasion or repressive cultural policies, from exerting their own authority as writers. Within the context of the Fascist regime, which censured female enterprises diverging from the maternal role, women's acts of writing, of putting their thoughts, emotions, and experiences to paper, may be read as a site of nonconformist ideology.

By reading women's literary texts and commentary against the responses of male critics we clearly see the difference of the poetics women elaborated. As stated above, the beginnings of women's own writing project predate Fascism, with the early efforts of such authors as Deledda, Negri, and Prosperi. For instance, in "Aridità sentimentale" (Emotional aridity, 1911), Guglielminetti urged female writers to exercise their authority on the subject of women's existence and to write about their own lives, speaking of what had been omitted in the discourses of science, history, and the arts. The points of variance between this emergent women's aesthetic and the dominant trend in Italian literature—which structure subsequent literary debates of the twenties and thirties—are described in an essay by Croce, the foremost theorist of "pure art." Croce's work on aesthetics, as critic and philosopher, exerted a formative influence on literary assessment of the interwar period. Locating women's writing within the context of modern literature, Croce maintains that female authors and poets writing at the turn of the century (many of whom are represented in this volume) constitute a new phenomenon in Italy, differing from the past when "rare voices broke with scholastic decorum and the imitation of literary models by speaking in female accents and passionate outpourings" ("Alinda Bonacci—Vittoria Aganoor—Enrichetta Capecelatro," 366). Despite individual differences among female writers, they all, Croce observes, "are directly inspired by the life they see around themselves and by the passions which stir them" (366). Tending not to write within established literary models, women's expressive forms possess "fire and color." While praising these innovations, Croce questions their critical and aesthetic foundation by attributing these new writing practices primarily to weak literary training. Thus, he perceives the trend among women writers to utilize a direct, unadorned language fashioned from the personal experience of daily living as a "lack" of stylistic polish.

By the twenties, the differences between women's practices of writing and those of their male counterparts comprised a major topic of critical debate, reflecting the general concern over gender difference in Italian society. Giuseppe Ravegnani provides a particularly important representation of how women's writing challenged the canon and traditional notions of woman in his 1930 study *Contemporanei* (Contemporary authors). While predictably defending the superior value of the male literary tradition, Ravegnani states that women's writing

> for the most part lives and nourishes itself on the margins of another greater, greatly more sober and conclusive literature. It seems to us . . . that female literature, particularly the recent one, likes putting on trousers, and has the mania of putting a mask of openness and even cynicism on its

face. . . . As for us, we would like a woman, especially if overflowing with ink, to be old-fashioned, perhaps romantic, homey, and a little exhausted by housework; that is to say, concerned with what may well be a world precluded to man's observation, frightened to offend and to pervert the nature of femininity's intimate secret. (55–6)[10]

Though Ravegnani locates women's literature in the margins of the dominant literary tradition, he creates a suggestive image of how it wears away the traditional boundaries between the masculine and feminine, while refusing to reproduce the conventional image of femininity. As illustrated by such stories as "Grace," "Man and Death," "The Captain," and "Sensitivity," women authors rewrite the cultural image of woman, representing new forms of female identity and desire. Furthermore, they openly examine crucial issues concerning the material and psychological conditions of female oppression—the objectification of women in society, the cultural ideal of female self-sacrifice, sexual abuse, and the economic problems of working women among the lower classes.

Although many critics applauded women's texts for their treatment of social issues (Deledda and Negri were both praised as antiliterary, socialistic writers), exponents of "pure art" engaged in a frequently emotional critique of women's writing practices prior to and during the interwar period. This trend may, I suggest, be read as a defensive response to the ways women's writing challenged male literary authority and exerted increasing influence among the reading public. Although diverse tendencies in literature and criticism did circulate during the years of Fascism, the aesthetic of "pure art" formed the primary reference for critics attempting to demonstrate the inferiority of women's literature. The two essays Croce devotes to Negri's poetry and prose explicate the central precepts of "pure art," while identifying the contending principles developed by Negri and other women writers. The characteristics Croce censures in Negri's writing in 1906—which include working through her life experience as a source of art, a commitment to social problems, and a lack of stylistic elaboration—form the central themes in discussions of women's literature conducted among proponents of "pure art" in the twenties and thirties. Croce admittedly adopts a position opposing that of the majority of critics and general readers, who acclaimed Negri's early poems as "an antiliterary, extremely sincere poetry constituted of real life" ("Ada Negri," 344). Writing from her experience, they maintain, Negri "speaks to us of the fears, hopes, and battles she has actually experienced and sustained . . . and she makes us feel the problems of tormented modern life" (344). Yet this assessment, Croce cautions, confuses the sincerity of the artist with "artistic sincerity." Arguing for the transcendence of art over personal experience, history, politics, and social conditions, Croce states that "the categorical imperative of the artist toward art is to make a beautiful work and nothing other than a beautiful work" (361). Thus Croce maintains that Negri's conception of writing as a social practice, a product of her "naive desire for goodness and justice," works against the pure artistic ideal since "every attempt to make art a mission kills art. Poetry is an end, not a means" (352).

Croce's later article on Negri, published in 1940, takes up issues examined in his earlier assessment, yet focuses more specifically on how Negri's style contests the "universal" as literary imperative. Croce does praise Negri for having achieved a certain "mastery" over her use of language. However, the source of Negri's later writing—composed of her "private self"—prevents her from truly attaining style, by which Croce means "pure poetry." Negri, Croce explains, "has found herself alone with her private 'I.' The poet must find himself alone with the universal 'I' and not with the private self, with humanity, which is totality, and not with his particular and personal needs, his adventures and misadventures, and pleasures and troubles which wound him as a practical man—all of which offer only the stimulus for finding the purely human" ("L'ultima Ada Negri" [Ada Negri's Later Work], 292).

While Croce accurately describes the difference between Negri's literary ideal and that prescribed by the aesthetic of "pure art," he mistakes her choice to write from a personal gendered position for a failure to attain "pure" poetic style, which cannot represent the female subject at all. The short stories Negri wrote during the twenties and thirties, including "The Captain" and "Woman with a Little Girl," are representative of the different aesthetic she and other female authors were elaborating. The imperatives of this aesthetic, also outlined by Guglielminetti, called for women to write their lives in their own words, and thus produce a document of "extraordinary truth." Formulating their own notion of artistic sincerity, female authors give literary expression to the ideas, emotions, and ambitions they have experienced or perceived, and create a public forum to share their consciousness of sexual difference and gender construction with other women. "No one has ever understood anything about us women and we have too much pride to scream our secret pain, naked and raw as it is," Negri discloses, "but if you entrust yourself to my heart, perhaps you will see your own in a mirror" ("Woman with a Little Girl," 91).

In general, as we see in "Sensitivity," "A White Cloud," and "A Life Story?," women writers favor collapsed or parallel histories, intimate conversations between women, and first person narratives to express their perceptions of what events and phases in the life-course may mean to women in patriarchal society. These systems of representation and address—in "Woman with a Little Girl" and "Man and Death" the narrators directly address the female reader—valorize women's ways of being and knowing as significant subjects for literature, while delegitimating the "objective" male authorial stance. In the twenties and thirties the tendency among female authors to write about women's lives from their personal experience was so diffuse that critics invariably categorized their literature as a form of "autobiographism." The distinct ways commentators deployed the term *autobiographism* clearly illustrate an alternate, transgressive kind of life writing formulated by women writers. While proponents of the transcendent and universal as artistic ideals applauded such writers as Giovanni Papini and Piero Jahier for their autobiographical musings on metaphysical and existential problems, displayed in a lyrical prose with stylistic brilliance, they employed this label to denote the different, and to them inferior, quality of women's literature. Today, our notion of autobiographism of the interwar period, for which women were infamous, derives almost exclusively from male texts.[11] Women's practices of autobiographism are critical for reassessing the ways female discourses and self-representations challenged the terms of masculine culture. The threats women's life-writing posed are exemplified by Camillo Pellizzi's observation that "the disease of autobiography is more dangerous and endemic among women writers" (*Le lettere italiane del nostro secolo,* [Italian literature of our century], 78).

Among some critics, the "unspeakably" intimate nature of women's literary subjects and the narrative forms created to address the reader evoked objections that such writing was too personal, sentimental, unreflective, and lacking in stylistic polish. Piero Gobetti for instance, complains that "A woman's novel—inevitably autobiographical—strives to reach the polite reader like a candid letter, strictly personal. . . . The character of exhibitionism which one wants to denounce in all female literature is almost always this innocent sharing of a confidence" ("Sibilla," 200). However, the heightened affective and expressive components of women's writing of this period may also be seen as attempts to break patriarchal control of language, culture, and society. Women's experimentation with forms of expression derives from the authors' desires to speak of themselves in ways never heard before, disclosing what had been repressed in the cultural image of woman. With few exceptions women writers reject the "high" literary language, which Antonio Gramsci and others have critiqued as an exclusionary address to the social elite. Such writers as Deledda, Guglielminetti, Negri, and Tartufari thus set their writing practices against dominant literary forms, creating a discursive space for dissent. Such politics of writing, which reached wide circulation in women's narratives published in the daily press, are especially important in the context of the Fascist dictatorship, whose policies were aimed at stifling all forms of opposition, cultural and otherwise.

It would be unwise, however, to minimize the struggles with language in which each author engaged to create her own voice. Certainly the language of writers represented in this collection is influenced by class, geographic location, education, and poetics. Manzini, for instance, relies somewhat more on traditional literary vocabulary to fashion her nuanced, and startling, visions of women's ways of knowing. Yet, as Piero Bigongiari notes in 1940, for Manzini "to write is to search for a way of speaking" (*Prosa per il Novecento* [Twentieth-century prose], 92). Deledda, on the other hand, had to learn "standard" Italian much like a foreign language. Both she and Negri experimented with linguistic forms throughout their careers, and received criticism for stylistic "imperfections"—in other words, for breaking the rules of "high" literary style. The different language usage in women's texts represents the authors' endeavors to fashion new ways to speak.[12] Furthermore, such unreceptive assessments reflect the inability of the critical establishment to value women's narrative innovations, not inferior literary abilities. Ravegnani advances a similar proposition in the case of Negri, suggesting that the style of her earlier poetry displays an uneasiness deriving from the "need to speak of herself," a need that also generates "the effort to create her own personal way of expressing herself" (*Contemporanei*, 84).

While such writers as Negri, Prosperi, and Tartufari strive to tell their stories of oppression, hope, and accomplishment in a candid, unadorned, yet highly expressive language, this does not mean that their narratives lack reflection, an ability Pellizzi claims "is perhaps alien to the gentle sex in general, for whom speculation is a luxury and almost, you might say, an anomaly" (*Le lettere italiane del nostro secolo*, 74). The difference between the notion of contemplation advanced by proponents of "pure art" and the terms of contemplation elaborated in women's narratives originates in their distinct aesthetics: writing as autonomous creative activity versus writing as social practice. Thus, most writers represented in this volume do not pause over the abstract or metaphysical problems of existence, or adopt an ostensibly "objective" position toward their subject. Nor do they claim the universal. Yet such stories as "Man and Death," "The Pomegranate," and "Woman with a Little Girl" are highly self-reflective, as they examine a different female subject and her conflicted relation to dominant cultural narratives of woman in Italian life and society. The heightened emotional power of women's narratives constitutes a significant element of their meaning, for emotion comes of the writers' struggles to express their intimate thoughts, feelings, conflicts, and desires, which cannot be contained.[13]

After nearly fifty years of critical neglect, the re-publication of the short stories in this volume has important implications for studies on Italian life and culture during Fascism, the tradition of Italian women's literature, and contemporary theories of literary production. The literature written by critically recognized and popular women authors tells us much about their own concerns, interests, and tastes, as well as those of the general reading public. By examining the forms of self-representation and expression women developed, we gain a more complex understanding of the broader ideological system and how women's writing contended with its dominant literary and social codes. Certainly the copius presence of women writers as the subjects of their literature and as the objects of critical debate belies the notion that the twenty years of Fascist rule represent a gap in the history of female storytelling. Furthermore, these narratives implicitly raise questions—about the categorization and canonization of works of art—which have been forestalled by suppressing the different literary project women formulated and realized during Fascism.

Notes

1. Among the few recent anthologies that record Clarice Tartufari's literary achievements are Natalia Costa-Zalessow, *Scrittrici italiane dal XIII al XX secolo* and Giuliana Morandini, *La voce che è in lei*.

2. Pia Rimini's name does appear on a list of authors of whom the Fascist government disapproved in 1940, which is reprinted in Philip V. Cannistraro, *La fabbrica del consenso* (The construction of consent), 432.

3. The subject of Italian women of the Renaissance has experienced a boom of interest, generating numerous articles and book-length studies, among them Marilyn Migiel and Juliana Schiesari, eds., *Refiguring Woman*; Margaret L. King and Albert Rabil, Jr., eds., *Her Immaculate Hand*; Patricia H. Labalme, *Beyond Their Sex*; and several substantive articles in *Annali d'Italianistica* 7 (1989), a volume devoted to Italian women's writing.

4. Giaime Pintor's description of how his experience of World War II changed his conception of the intellectual's role in society appears in a letter he wrote to his brother a few days before dying in an attempt to reach the partisans in central Italy.

5. In contrast to other genres of women's writing popular during Fascism, the romance novel of the twenties and thirties has received much critical attention. For a substantive bibliography see *Intorno al rosa*, edited

by the Centro Di Documentazione, Ricerca Ed Iniziativa Delle Donne.

6. With few embellishments, this literary script, which has gained authority through repetition, is played out with a stable cast of "major" and "minor" male authors in the sixties and seventies in such studies as *A Guide to Contemporary Italian Literature* (1962) by Sergio Pacifici; the chapter on realist writers in the 1967 study, *Storia della letteratura italiana contemporanea (1940–1965)* by Giuliano Manacorda; and *The Seizure of Power* (1973) by Adrian Lyttelton. The outlook is no less bleak in anthologies and critical studies of the eighties. Although the 1984 collection of critical essays *La cultura italiana negli anni 1930–1945* (Italian culture from 1930–1945) unites some fifty-five studies on a broad range of cultural topics, none examines the subject of women's literature. The only essay on a female figure concerns Margherita Sarfatti's accomplishments in the visual arts. Salvatore Guglielmino does not include any women writers in the section on the interwar period in his 1984 anthology *Guida al Novecento* (Guide to the Twentieth century), but a selection by Gianna Manzini somehow meets Mario Pazzaglia's criteria, making her the sole woman writer among twenty-one male writers representing the interwar years in *Letteratura italiana* (Italian literature) III (1986). Surprisingly, Pazzaglia does not include any selection by Deledda, despite her 1926 Nobel Prize. Equally puzzling is Lino Pertile's silence on women writers in his 1986 article "Fascism and Literature," broken only to mention Liala, an author of romance fiction who enjoyed explosive popularity during Fascism.

7. For a detailed study of the linguistic innovations in women's texts of the twenties see Daniela Curti's "Il linguaggio del racconto rosa" (The language of the romance story).

8. The approach Paola Blelloch adopts toward women's writing of the Fascist period in *Quel mondo dei guanti e delle stoffe* (That world of gloves and fabrics) is representative of this tendency. She maintains that there are two distinct periods in twentieth-century women's literature, the years from 1900 to 1925 and the time from 1950 on, that are separated by a "hiatus" during Fascism, spanning the years from 1925 to 1945 (14–16). Blelloch's primary source for this conclusion is Maria Antonietta Macciocchi's study *La donna "nera"* (The woman in black), which continues to structure how literary commentators think about women writing during the dictatorship. Although Macciocchi's 1976 analysis merits attention for what it reveals about woman in Fascist ideology, by focusing on dominant discourses and policies designed to engineer female consent it prevents us from seeing women's oppositional discourses and practices, as I have argued in "Unseduced Mothers."

9. In *Il Novecento letterario in Italia* (Twentieth-Century literature in Italy) II, Giuseppe Petronio and Luciana Martinelli describe important cultural changes of the twenties and thirties that contributed to the growth

of the publishing market for women. These include "the development . . . of a technological civilization, the broad increase in literacy, the
initial formation of a publishing industry, the birth of a mass society, the
emancipation of women along American models, the formation of a wide
group of professions entrusted to women and requiring a certain level of
culture" (359). Within the specific context of the cultural page in the daily
press, the mid-twenties saw a notable increase in the publication of wom-
en's literature by acclaimed and popular writers. In 1936 Maria Castellani,
director of the Fascist Professional Women's Association, estimated that
there were some 391 Italian women writers and journalists (Alexander De
Grand, "Women under Italian Fascism," *The Historical Journal* 19(4): 960),
while Stanis Ruinas arrives at a higher estimate of over 500 female authors
in *Scrittrici e scribacchine d'oggi* (Women writers and scribblers of today),
published in 1930. For a detailed historical study of publication practices
in the Italian women's press during Fascism see Elisabetta Mondello, *La
nuova italiana.*

10. The translation of this passage is drawn from Sergio Pacifici's ren-
dering of Ravegnani's assessment in *The Modern Italian Novel from Capuana
to Tozzi,* 49. I have however changed antiquated terminology, for example
"female literature" is substituted for "feminine literature," and I have re-
stored some images to their literal form where I thought meaning had been
lost.

11. For representative analyses of male autobiographism and its con-
ventions from 1900 to 1940, see Clelia Martignoni, "Per una storia dell'autobiografismo metafisico vociano" and Paolo Briganti, "La cerchia infuocata."

12. Mario Aste, in *Grazia Deledda,* 12–13, provides a thoughtful reas-
sessment of Deledda's style, locating her writing in the linguistic tradition
of Sardinia.

13. Useful here is the formulation of the melodramatic mode provided by Peter Brooks in *The Melodramatic Imagination,* which, through its
heightened expressivity, represents the "essential conflicts of daily living"
(3). "The desire to express all," Brooks argues, "seems a fundamental characteristic of the melodramatic mode. Nothing is spared because nothing is
left unsaid; the characters stand on stage and utter the unspeakable, give
voice to their deepest feelings, dramatize through their heightened and
polarized words and gestures the whole lesson of their relationship" (4).

Works Cited

AA.VV. *Intorno al rosa*. Ed. Centro Di Documentazione Ricerca Ed Iniziativa Delle Donne. Verona: Essedue, 1987.

AA.VV. *La cultura italiana negli anni 1930–1945*. 2 vols. Napoli: Edizioni Italiane, 1984.

Aste, Mario. *Grazia Deledda: Ethnic Novelist*. Potomac, Md.: Scripta Humanistica, 1990.

Balducci, Carolyn. *A Self-Made Woman: Biography of Nobel-Prize-Winner Grazia Deledda*. Boston: Houghton Mifflin, 1975.

Bigongiari, Piero. *Prosa per il Novecento*. Firenze: La Nuova Italia, 1970.

Birnbaum, Lucia Chiavola. *Liberazione della donna: Feminism in Italy*. Middletown: Wesleyan University Press, 1986.

Blelloch, Paola. *Quel mondo dei guanti e delle stoffe . . . : Profili di scrittrici italiane del '900*. Verona: Essedue, 1987.

Briganti, Paolo. "La cerchia infuocata. Per una tipologia dell'autobiografia letteraria italiana del Novecento." *Annali d'Italianistica* 4 (1986): 189–222.

Brooks, Peter. *The Melodramatic Imagination: Balzac, Henry James, Melodrama, and the Mode of Excess*. New Haven: Yale University Press, 1976.

Caldwell, Lesley. "Reproducers of the Nation: Women and the Family in Fascist Policy." *Rethinking Italian Fascism: Capitalism, Populism and Culture*. Edited by David Forgacs. London: Lawrence and Wisehart, 1986, 110–41.

Cannistraro, Philip V. *La fabbrica del consenso: Fascismo e mass media*. Bari: Laterza, 1975.

Costa-Zalessow, Natalia. *Scrittrici italiane dal XIII al XX secolo: Testi e critica.* Ravenna: Longo, 1982.

Croce, Benedetto. "Ada Negri" and "Alinda Bonacci, Vittoria Aganoor, Enrichetta Capecelatro." *La letteratura della nuova Italia: Saggi critici.* 5th ed. Vol. 2. Bari: Laterza, 1948, 344–65 and 366–90.

_____. "L'ultima Ada Negri." *La letteratura della nuova Italia: Saggi critici.* Vol. 6. Bari: Laterza, 1940, 291–301.

Curti, Daniela. "Il linguaggio del racconto rosa: Gli anni 20 ed oggi." In *Lingua letteraria e lingua dei media nell'italiano contemporaneo.* Firenze: Felice Le Monnier, 1987, 156–73.

De Felice, Renzo. *Interpretations of Fascism.* Translated by Brenda Huff Everett. Cambridge: Harvard University Press, 1977.

De Giovanni, Neria. *L'ora di Lilith: Su Grazia Deledda e la letteratura femminile del secondo Novecento.* Roma: Ellemme, 1987.

De Grand, Alexander. *Italian Fascism: Its Origins and Development.* 2nd ed. Lincoln: University of Nebraska Press, 1982.

_____. "Women Under Italian Fascism." *The Historical Journal.* 19(4) (1976), 947–68.

De Grazia, Victoria. *The Culture of Consent: Mass Organization of Leisure in Fascist Italy.* Cambridge: Cambridge University Press, 1981.

_____. *How Fascism Ruled Women: Italy, 1922–1945.* Berkeley: University of California Press, 1992.

Flora, Francesco. *Note di servizio.* Milano: Mondadori, 1945.

Forgacs, David, ed. *Rethinking Italian Fascism: Capitalism, Populism and Culture.* London: Lawrence and Wishart, 1986.

Giocondi, Michele. *Lettori in camicia nera: Narrativa di successo nell'Italia fascista.* Messina-Firenze: G. D'Anna, 1978.

Gobetti, Piero. "Sibilla." In *Sibilla Aleramo e il suo tempo: Vita raccontata e illustrata,* edited by Bruna Conti and Alba Morino. Milano: Feltrinelli, 1981, 200–201.

Gramsci, Antonio. *Selections from Cultural Writings.* Translated by William Boelhower. Edited by David Forgacs and Geoffrey Nowell-Smith. London: Lawrence and Wishart, 1985.

Guglielminetti, Amalia. "Aridità sentimentale." *La stampa.* 11 July 1911.

Guglielminetti, Marziano. *Amalia: La rivincita della femmina.* Genova: Costa and Nolan, 1987.

Guglielmino, Salvatore. *Guida al Novecento: Profilo letterario e antologia.* 4th ed. Milano: Principato, 1987.

King, Margaret L. and Albert Rabil Jr., eds. *Her Immaculate Hand: Selected Works by and about the Women Humanists of Quattrocento Italy.* Binghamton: Center for Medieval and Early Renaissance Studies, State University of New York at Binghamton, 1983.

Labalme, Patricia H. *Beyond Their Sex: Learned Women of the European Past.* New York: New York University Press, 1980.

Lyttelton, Adrian. *The Seizure of Power: Fascism in Italy 1919–1929.* New York: Charles Scribner's Sons, 1973.

Macciocchi, Maria Antonietta. *La donna "nera": "Consenso" femminile e fascismo.* Milano: Feltrinelli, 1976.

Manacorda, Giuliano. *Storia della letteratura italiana contemporanea (1940–1965).* 3rd. ed. Roma: Riuniti, 1974.

_____. *Storia della letteratura italiana tra le due guerre 1919–1943.* Roma: Riuniti, 1980.

Martignoni, Clelia. "Per una storia dell'autobiografismo metafisico vociano." *Autografo* 1(2) (1984): 32–47.

Meldini, Piero. *Sposa e madre esemplare: Ideologia e politica della donna e della famiglia durante il fascismo.* Firenze: Guaraldi, 1975.

Miceli-Jeffries, Giovanna. "Gianna Manzini's Poetics of Verbal Visualization." *Contemporary Women Writers in Italy: A Modern Renaissance.* Edited by Santo L. Aricò. Amherst: University of Massachusetts Press, 1990.

Migiel, Marilyn and Juliana Schiesari, eds. *Refiguring Woman: Perspectives on Gender in the Italian Renaissance.* Ithaca, NY: Cornell University Press, 1991.

Mondello, Elisabetta. *La nuova italiana: La donna nella stampa e nella cultura del ventennio.* Roma: Riuniti, 1987.

Morandini, Giuliana. *La voce che è in lei: Antologia della narrativa femminile italiana tra '800 e '900.* Milano: Bompiani, 1980.

Negri, Ada. *Tutte le opere di Ada Negri.* 2nd. ed. 2 vols. Milano: Mondadori, 1966.

Ojetti, Ugo. "Ada Negri." *Cose viste.* Milano: Treves, 1923–1939.

Pacifici, Sergio. *A Guide to Contemporary Italian Literature: Futurism to Neorealism.* New York: Meridian, 1962.

_____. *The Modern Italian Novel: From Capuana to Tozzi.* Carbondale: Southern Illinois University Press, 1973.

Parsani, M. Assunta and Neria De Giovanni. *Femminile a confronto, tre realtà della narrativa contemporanea: Alba De Céspedes, Fausta Cialente, Gianna Manzini.* Manduria-Bari-Roma: Lacaita, 1984.

Passerini, Luisa. *Fascism in Popular Memory: The Cultural Experience of the Turin Working Class,* translated by Robert Lumley and Jude Bloomfield. Cambridge: Cambridge University Press, 1987.

Pazzaglia, Mario. *Letteratura italiana: Testi e critica con lineamenti di storia letteraria.* 2nd ed. 3 vols. Firenze: Zanichelli, 1986.

Pellizzi, Camillo. *Le lettere italiane del nostro secolo.* Milano: Libreria d'Italia, 1929.

Pertile, Lino. "Fascism and Literature." *Rethinking Italian Fascism: Capital-*

ism, Populism and Culture, edited by David Forgacs. London: Lawrence and Wishart, 1986, 162–84.

Petronio, Giuseppe and Luciana Martinelli. *Il Novecento letterario in Italia: I contemporanei.* Palermo: Palumbo, 1975.

Pintor, Giaime. *Il sangue d'Europa.* Torino: Einaudi, 1965.

Ravegnani, Giuseppe. *Contemporanei: Dal tramonto dell'Ottocento all'alba del Novecento.* Torino: Fratelli Bocca, 1930.

Ruinas, Stanis. *Scrittrici e scribacchine d'oggi.* Roma: Accademia, 1930.

Saba, Marina Addis, ed. *La corporazione delle donne: Ricerche e studi sui modelli femminili nel ventennio fascista.* Firenze: Vallecchi, 1988.

Schnapp, Jeffrey and Barbara Spackman, eds. *Stanford Italian Review.* 8 (1988).

Tannenbaum, Edward R. *The Fascist Experience: Italian Society and Culture 1922–1945.* New York: Basic Books, 1972.

Vittorini, Elio. *In Sicily. A Vittorini Omnibus.* New York: New Directions, 1960.

West, Rebecca, and Dino S. Cervigni, eds. *Annali d'Italianistica* 7: Women's Voices in Italian Literature (1989).

Wilhelm, Maria de Blasio. *The Other Italy: The Italian Resistance in World War II.* New York: W. W. Norton and Company, 1988.

Whitfield, John Humphreys. *A Short History of Italian Literature.* 2nd ed. Manchester: Manchester University Press, 1980.

The Feminist Press at The City University of New York offers alternatives in education and in literature. Founded in 1970, this nonprofit, tax-exempt educational and publishing organization works to eliminate stereotypes in books and schools and to provide literature with a broad vision of human potential. The publishing program includes reprints of important works by women, feminist biographies of women, multicultural anthologies, a cross-cultural memoir series, and nonsexist children's books. Curricular materials, bibliographies, directories, and a quarterly journal provide information and support for students and teachers of women's studies. Through publications and projects, The Feminist Press contributes to the rediscovery of the history of women and the emergence of a more humane society.

New and Forthcoming Books from The Feminist Press

Anna Teller, a novel by Jo Sinclair. Afterword by Anne Halley. $35.00 cloth, $16.95 paper.
Changes, a novel by Ama Ata Aidoo. Afterword by Tuzyline Allan. $35.00 cloth, $12.95 paper.
Fault Lines, a memoir by Meena Alexander. $35.00 cloth, $12.95 paper.
Get Smart! What You Should Know (But Won't Learn in Class) about Sexual Harassment and Sexual Discrimination, second edition, by Montana Katz and Veronica Vieland. $35.00 cloth, $12.95 paper.
Proud Man, a novel by Katharine Burdekin (Murray Constantine). Foreword and afterword by Daphne Patai. $35.00 cloth, $14.95 paper.
The Seasons: Death and Transfiguration, a memoir by Jo Sinclair. $35.00 cloth, $12.95 paper.
Women Composers: The Lost Tradition Found, second edition, by Diane Peacock Jezic. Foreword by Elizabeth Wood. Second edition prepared by Elizabeth Wood. $35.00 cloth, $14.95 paper.
Women Writing in India: 600 B.C. to the Present. Volume I: 600 B.C. to the Early Twentieth Century. Volume II: The Twentieth Century. Edited by Susie Tharu and K. Lalita. Each volume $59.95 cloth, $29.95 paper.

Prices subject to change. Individuals: send prepaid book orders to The Feminist Press at The City University of New York, 311 East 94 Street, New York, NY 10128. Please include $3.00 postage and handling for the first book, $.75 for each additional. Feminist Press titles are distributed to the trade by Consortium Book Sales & Distribution, (800) 283-3572.